The
Wishcatchers

The Wishcatchers

CAROL CHRISTIE

 Kelpies

Kelpies is an imprint of Floris Books

First published in 2011 by Floris Books

The publisher acknowledges subsidy from
Creative Scotland towards the publication
of this volume.

Mixed Sources
Product group from well-managed
forests and other controlled sources
www.fsc.org Cert no. TT-COC-2139
© 1996 Forest Stewardship Council
FSC

British Library CIP Data available
ISBN 978-086315-801-8
Printed in Great Britain
by CPI Cox & Wyman

For Emily and Andrew

With thanks to Clare Whittaker, who was in on the Wishcatchers from the very start, and to Alistair, who told me to follow my dreams.

Chapter 1

Ant stuffed a chocolate-spread sandwich into her pocket and grabbed her water bottle. "See you later, Mum."

"Where are you off to?"

Ant shrugged. "Just out."

"Don't let me find you've been out to Wishcatchers' Point again. You've set your wish. Now just leave it. You know what Gran always says ..."

"I know. I know. 'A watched wish is seldom granted.' I'll probably go down to the beach."

"Don't be late back," said her mum. "Dinner's at six."

Ant slammed the door and set off down the path. At the end of the street she hesitated. She really had meant to go out to Wishcatchers' Point.

Across the street, Rosie Brash was sitting on the wall of the park with her friends. "Ooh, look who it is!" she called. "I bet I know where you're going. Off to Wishcatchers' Point to wish to be normal like everyone else." Rosie's friends giggled.

That did it – there was no way she could go to the point now. Ant stuck her hands in her pockets and headed in the opposite direction, ignoring the sniggers and whispers behind her.

She walked right to the end of the beach, paddling in the shallow water. Then she put her trainers back on and scrambled over the rocks into the next bay and beyond.

Ant's scuffing feet sent pebbles scuttling towards the sea as she made her way across the stony beach. She'd been out for hours now – she was at least three miles from the village and she'd come the hard way over the rocks from inlet to inlet. Nobody else ever came that way – even at low tide there were places where you had to wade through water up to your knees.

Luckily she was wearing shorts so her legs had dried quickly, although her feet still squelched in her trainers. She munched her chocolate-spread sandwich and wished she'd brought another drink. The water in her bottle was long finished. She wiped her hands on her shorts and squinted out to sea. The tide had turned an hour ago. She'd need to be getting back soon.

Ahead of her was a tall rock shaped like an elephant, which she'd never been up before. She would climb it and then start back. If the tide was too far in by then, she could scramble up to the cliff path and go back that way. She unscrewed the top of her water bottle to get the very last drip of moisture out, tipping her head right back to feel the miserly dribble on her tongue. Then she put the lid back on, shoved the bottle into the pocket of her hoodie and set off purposefully towards the elephant rock.

As she got closer, she could see that where the trunk of the elephant curled round towards the body there was a dark patch, as though there might be an opening. She made straight for it, climbing swiftly, almost without thinking, handhold, foothold, handhold, foothold.

Just below the mouth of the opening she stopped and peered in. It was too dark to see anything much. Hoisting herself up on her elbows, she crawled through. The opening was low and narrow, but Ant was skinny and slipped through it easily. Once inside she found she could stand. Waiting for her eyes to adjust to the darkness, she stretched out her arms, trying to work out the size of the cave. To her left and right she could feel rough walls of rock, but when she reached out in front she felt nothing but air.

Little by little, as her eyes got used to the dimness, she could make out more. The cave was not completely dark. Some light leaked in from the opening through which she had come, but she realised there must be a hole somewhere in the roof too, because there was light filtering through further into the cave. She took a couple of steps, careful not to stumble on any rocky bumps, but the floor seemed surprisingly smooth. She bent down to touch it and felt dry, silky stone, like the worn flagstones in her gran's kitchen.

The silvery, slithery sound of running water made her remember how thirsty she was. Turning her head from side to side she tried to work out where the noise was coming from. She walked towards the back of the cave, following the sound. The rocky walls made a funnel shape, pulling her close in, drawing her forwards. She had to tuck her arms into her sides so she didn't get stuck. Just as she thought it was getting too narrow to go any further, the cave twisted to the right.

Ant blinked against the light. After a moment or two she could see that it was coming down in a great shaft from a gap in the rock overhead. The light fell on a little waterfall, which glistened and glinted, splurging and splashing into a natural bowl in the rock. She went closer. Where the cascade entered the pool, the water swirled and dimpled, but closer to the edge, the pool was still. Tentatively, Ant put a finger into the water, making a ripple in the perfect surface. It was cold. She put the finger to her lips. Fresh water. She'd known it wouldn't be salt – the sea wouldn't reach as high as this, even at a spring tide.

There was a hollow in the rock beside the pool, just the right size and height to make a seat, so Ant sat and watched the water spilling down. She wondered why the pool didn't overflow when so much water was constantly pattering into it. There must be an outlet somewhere she couldn't see, deep in the rock. The pool was constantly being refreshed, the water flowing out being replaced with water flowing in. That's why it was so clear and clean – perfectly good for drinking.

She leaned over the rocky basin, filled her cupped hands and drank. The icy-cold water made her gasp but the feel of it on her parched tongue was good. She drank again and again, then sat back and wiped her mouth on her sleeve.

The pool was no more than ten or fifteen centimetres deep and she could clearly see the ridges on a pearly-white dog-whelk shell which lay on the sandy bottom. A glint caught her eye. There was something else in the water, tucked under the shell. She dipped her hand into the pool and pulled out a silver chain. The shell came too, strung on the chain like a pendant. She laid the necklace out in her palm. The catch was broken. She wondered who it belonged to and how long it had been lost.

Ant imagined a girl coming into the cave, just as she had, and stopping to look into the pool. The girl couldn't have known that the clasp on her necklace was broken and couldn't have noticed it slip off and slide into the water. The girl, whoever she was, must have been quite careless, Ant thought. The necklace must have made a splash as it went in. She couldn't have been paying attention – or maybe something had distracted her.

A draught came from nowhere and chilled the back of Ant's neck. She took out her penknife and with the tip of its blade fixed the clasp. She put the necklace on, tucking it inside her t-shirt. Immediately she felt a warm, soothing sensation flooding through her body.

She should be getting back. The tide must be well on its way in now.

After the quiet and dim of the cave, the shock of the harsh sunlight and crashing waves made her stumble. The sea was almost at the high-tide mark. She must have been in the cave much longer than she'd thought. Now it was impossible to go back the way she had come. She touched the shell around her neck, re-tied the loose lace of her left trainer and started to scramble up the cliff.

When she reached the path, she turned and looked back at the beach. From here, she couldn't see the cave. She couldn't even tell which was the elephant-shaped rock. Stuffing her hands into the pockets of her shorts, she began the long walk home.

Chapter 2

Ant kicked a stone against the bike-shed wall, head down, making herself as small as possible. She didn't kick the stone hard, so it only made a small *tut* noise as it hit the wooden wall of the shed. *Tut, tut, tut.* Surely it must be time for the bell.

She didn't dare look at her watch. The hands on it seemed to go so slowly during break, much more slowly than when she was in the classroom and a million times more slowly than when she was at home or out on the beach. Looking at her watch would only make time drag even more.

If she kept quiet and still it would be all right. If she didn't look up, nobody would notice she was there.

"Look who's here!" It was the unmistakable, shrill voice of Rosie Brash.

Ant knew it would be worse if she didn't answer. She took a moment to catch the stone under her foot, trapping it there, then she mumbled, "Hello, Rosie."

In a split second, Rosie was bent down beside her,

so close that Ant could feel her breath hot on her cheek. "What are you doing?"

Ant shrugged. "Just hanging about."

Rosie straightened and turned to address her friends. "Did you hear that? Antonia is just hanging about. We can't have that, can we?" She turned back to Ant. "Didn't Mrs Cook just give us a little talk about being nice to each other and all playing together?"

Ant shrugged again.

Rosie held out a hand. "Why don't you come and play with us?" Her voice was false and sickly sweet.

"Maybe in a minute," said Ant, feeling the bump of the stone under the sole of her school shoe. Surely the bell would go soon.

"Now!" commanded Rosie, and Sarah sniggered.

"OK." Ant tried to sound calm, but her heart was beating loudly as she followed Rosie into the middle of the playground.

Rosie stopped. Ant waited, trying not to think about what Rosie was planning. Whatever it was, it was probably worse than anything Ant could imagine.

"We'll play sleeping princesses," Rosie said eventually. "You be the princess." She shoved Ant into the middle.

"I want to be the princess," complained Rachel.

"It's Antonia's turn." Ant hated the way Rosie said her name, as though she couldn't quite believe it, each syllable carefully separated – An-to-ni-a. "Close your eyes," Rosie said. "No, tighter."

Ant screwed up her eyes.

"Tighter!" Rosie sighed. "That's no good. We're going to have to use your tie, Sarah."

Sarah was the only girl in the class who ever wore a shirt and school tie. Everybody else wore school polo shirts. Somehow, Sarah never got teased about it and the tie seemed to come in handy for a lot of Rosie's games. Now, Sarah wordlessly removed the tie and handed it to Rosie, who wound it roughly over Ant's eyes.

"There!" said Rosie.

She had tied it so tightly that Ant saw stars.

Rosie spun Ant around, making her dizzy. "Now, An-to-ni-a, see if you can catch us before we get to you."

As usual, Rosie was playing her own version of the game. It wasn't just the addition of the blindfold and the spinning. The girls didn't take turns to approach the sleeping princess and they didn't start far enough away. Instead they rushed at Ant all at once, not giving her a chance to point them out before they reached her. And instead of just tapping her when they got close, they slapped her on the back or on her arm, hard enough for Ant to wince at each blow. Someone, probably Rosie, pulled her hair.

Ant stood her ground. It was a matter of principle not to cry. Under her shirt she felt the shell necklace. It was smooth and warm against her skin. She could deal with this, she thought. In her head, she saw a seagull soaring high up above the sea and then swooping down again. It was almost restful, thinking of the seagull and the sound of the waves tugging and sucking at the sand.

The bell rang.

Ant heard the other children hurrying to line up. Nobody untied her blindfold. She reached up and fumbled for the knot. It was so tight that she struggled

15

to undo it. In the end, she had to work the tie loose and slide it off her head. She ran to join the back of her line.

"Last again, Antonia," said Mrs Cook disapprovingly.

"Sorry," said Ant.

When they got into the classroom, Rosie stuck up her hand.

"What is it, Rosie?" asked Mrs Cook.

"An-to-ni-a's got Sarah's tie."

Mrs Cook looked at Ant. Ant held out the tie.

"What on earth are you doing with Sarah's tie?" asked Mrs Cook wearily.

Ant shrugged.

Mrs Cook raised her eyebrows. "Answer me, please, Antonia."

Ant said, "I don't know."

Mrs Cook took the tie and gave it back to Sarah. "One hundred lines for tomorrow, please, Antonia. 'I must not take other people's property.'" Sarah sniggered and Mrs Cook said, "And I'll have a hundred lines from you too, Sarah. 'I must not laugh at other people's misfortune.'"

Sarah looked outraged.

"I bet she can't even spell misfortune," muttered Nichol, who sat at the desk next to Ant's.

Ant couldn't help giving a little smile. She sat down and opened her pencil case.

"Now," said Mrs Cook, "I have some news for you all." She looked about the classroom at the children's expectant faces. "We are going to have a new girl in the class. She'll be joining us tomorrow. Her name is Clarissa Wentworth."

"What kind of name is that?" hissed Rosie to Sarah.

Mrs Cook glared at Rosie before continuing. "And I'm sure I don't need to remind you to be kind to Clarissa. It's not easy being the new girl."

Mrs Cook started to talk about fractions. Ant sat at her desk and copied down sums, wondering what the new girl would be like and where she had come from. And then an idea began to form in her head. An idea that took hold and wouldn't go away.

Chapter 3

Clarissa stood with her arms folded as the removal men carried in boxes. From the labels she could see they were meant for the kitchen. Her mum had written on all the boxes, in giant black letters, KIT for the kitchen, SIT for the sitting room, CLA for Clarissa's room. She had used Clarissa's marker pen, without even asking. Now Clarissa thought gloomily that she'd probably never get her pen back. Even if her mum had remembered to pack it, it was just one small item in their massive whole house removal.

Clarissa scowled as she watched the men going in and out, with box after box full of kitchen things, pots and pans, plates and cups, cutlery and wooden spoons and cake tins and goodness knows what else. When they'd been packing up, her dad had said, "I can't believe we've got all this stuff! Do we really have to move it all?" Her mum had just said, "Yes" in her don't-argue-with-me voice and they had both gone back to wrapping glasses in newspaper.

The men disappeared into the removal lorry to drink from their flasks and read their newspapers. From inside the house, Clarissa could hear her dad shouting to Olivia to keep Tristan out of the kitchen. The unfamiliar path under Clarissa's feet felt lumpy and she curled up her toes in her old sandals.

"Are you just going to stand there?" said her mum, bringing out empty boxes. She looked funny with a dark smudge on one cheek and her hair tied back in a long scarf, which Clarissa hadn't seen before. She expertly ripped the packing tape from the boxes and flattened them, piling them neatly against the wall of the new house. After a while she stopped and looked at Clarissa. "Well?"

"What?"

"Aren't you going to go in and sort your room out? Nearly all your furniture's in. You could make a start on unpacking your clothes."

"Do I have to?"

Her mum wiped her forehead with a grubby hand, adding another smudge above her eyes. "You don't exactly have to. But you'll need to do it some time."

Clarissa looked away. "I don't feel like it," she said.

Her mum sighed. "Sweetheart, I know you didn't want us to move, but we had to. We're here now and you're going to have to accept it."

"I don't have to," said Clarissa. She walked out of the garden, narrowly avoiding a removal man carrying Tristan's sandpit. She heard her mum calling after her, but she pretended not to hear.

Clarissa had no idea where she was going. She'd only been in the village once before, the day they came to look at the house and she'd refused to get out of the car. Instead, she had curled up on the back seat and read *The Secret Garden* for what seemed like hours.

Anyway, it didn't matter where she went. She would need to walk for weeks to get where she really wanted to be – back home, in the house where she'd always lived, with her friends nearby. Clarissa tried not to cry as she walked, but she couldn't help it. The tears blurred her vision, but she still kept on going.

After a while, she got a stitch and stopped. Holding her side and taking deep breaths, she looked around. It seemed that she had walked right out of the village without noticing. She was on a grassy hill, looking towards the sea. She glared at the sea. How dare it sit there so blue and flat and calm!

The hill dipped gently towards the sea and then seemed to stop abruptly. She wondered if there was a cliff and walked a little way down to see. But the slope just got steeper and led down to some rocks and a little shaley beach. A dark green rowing boat had been tied to one of the rocks. It bobbed up and down with the waves.

Clarissa sat down on the grass and looked out to sea. After a while, she noticed that there was somebody on the beach, sitting cross-legged near the boat. She put a hand up to shield her eyes from the light and squinted at the person. It looked like a girl, probably not much older than she was. Clarissa wondered what she was doing.

Down on the beach, Ant tried to ignore the sharp bits of flint and stone that were jagging into her bare legs. If she sat very still and didn't wriggle, it was better, although she knew that she would still have pockmarked skin when she stood up. A gull swooped low across the sea, calling harshly. A fly buzzed nearby, but it wasn't the biting kind, so she just ignored it, even when it settled on her foot.

Ant looked down at her piece of paper and frowned. She knew what she wanted to wish for, but she couldn't quite think how to phrase it best.

She put the end of her pencil in her mouth and chewed it. The pencil didn't taste very nice and her mum and Mrs Cook were always on at her to stop doing it, but there was something about the gnawing of her teeth on the softening wood that helped her to concentrate.

After a while, she began to write, slowly and thoughtfully. For a wish to come true the way you wanted it to, you had to be careful how you worded it.

She wrote:

Dear Wishcatchers,

I wish that Rosie Brash would find someone else to pick on. There is a new girl coming to our class. I wish that Rosie would pick on her instead of me.

Love,
Ant

Once she had finished, Ant read through the letter. She felt a bit queasy. Maybe she was hungry. After school she'd gone straight down to get the boat, without having her usual snack. She folded up the paper, sealed it in a plastic box and put it into the creel she'd taken from the harbour-side earlier.

When she stood up, she had pins and needles and her legs felt rough where the stones had jabbed into them. She took a moment to shake out her legs and stamp the pins and needles away, then packed the creel into the boat and rowed off to set her wish.

As the boat moved away from the beach, Ant saw that there was someone sitting on the hillside. The sun was in her eyes, so she couldn't be sure, but it didn't look like anyone she knew. A sharp feeling of panic grabbed her. Was it the new girl?

Ant didn't want to think about that. She rowed faster than ever towards Wishcatchers' Point. When she got there, she hauled the weighted creel onto the side of the boat and dropped it into the water, without giving herself time to think. She watched until the bob of the marker buoy told her the creel had hit the bottom before rowing swiftly back to the harbour.

Chapter 4

Ant sat at her desk, doodling on the inside cover of her jotter. She had completed the worksheet on fractions ages ago, but she didn't want the others in the class to know she was first finished. It would only lead to trouble with Rosie later.

There was a knock at the classroom door and Mrs Hardcastle, the head teacher, came in, followed by a girl with blonde curly hair and the wrong school uniform.

The children put down their pencils and waited.

"Good morning, children," said Mrs Hardcastle.

"Good morning, Mrs Hardcastle."

"Children, I would like you to meet Clarissa Wentworth. She will be joining your class. I want you all to make Clarissa very welcome."

The children stared. Why was Clarissa wearing a blue sweatshirt instead of a red one? Hadn't anyone told her what the proper uniform was? Clarissa stared back at them. She didn't smile, but she didn't looked daunted either.

Mrs Cook was saying hello to Clarissa and introducing herself. Clarissa actually put out her hand for Mrs Cook to shake. The children stared all the more. Even Mrs Cook looked a bit surprised.

"You can sit here, next to Nichol," said Mrs Cook.

Clarissa said, "Thank you," and sat down. She opened her schoolbag and took out her pencil case and water bottle and laid them on her desk as if she had always sat there. Then she tucked her schoolbag under her desk and sat back in her seat.

Mrs Cook and Mrs Hardcastle had gone out into the corridor, leaving the door open. They were talking in low voices.

The children began to whisper among themselves, the noise starting off quietly but growing as they got more excited. They didn't know what to make of this new girl.

Clarissa sat in her seat, staring ahead, her back straight, her hands folded on the desk. For a while nobody included her in their whispered conversations, but then Nichol turned to her and asked the question they all wanted to ask.

"Why are you wearing the wrong uniform?"

"It wasn't the wrong uniform at St Mary's," said Clarissa stiffly.

"Is that your old school?" asked Nichol.

Clarissa didn't like the idea of St Mary's being her *old* school. She wanted it to be her *now* school. But she didn't want to explain all that to Nichol. Instead she just nodded.

"But you will get the right uniform?" said Nichol. "Everybody has to wear our uniform."

"In due course," said Clarissa. It was what her dad had told her this morning, as her mum tried to persuade her to wear a red cardigan instead of her St Mary's sweatshirt.

"You don't want to look out of place," her mum had said, holding up the red cardigan. "I've ordered you a new uniform, but it won't come until after the holidays. Put this on and you'll blend in more."

"Maybe I don't want to blend in," said Clarissa, feeling her face going as red as the cardigan.

"You'll get your new uniform in due course," said her dad firmly, lacing up his shoes. "And then you'll have to wear it."

"But I don't have it now and I want to wear my St Mary's sweatshirt."

Olivia, Clarissa's older sister, went past, neatly buttoned into her own red cardigan. She said airily, "You always have to make a mountain out of a molehill, Clarissa." Her mum sighed. But Clarissa got to wear her blue sweatshirt.

Of course, Clarissa didn't tell her new classmates any of this, or that she fully intended to keep her St Mary's uniform on for the rest of the term.

Mrs Cook came back into the room. "What's all this chat? Don't you have work to do?"

The children took up their pencils again and went back to their fractions. Mrs Cook got Clarissa a jotter and worksheet and explained to her what they were doing.

Clarissa interrupted her. "It's all right, Mrs Cook. I did all about fractions at St Mary's." She took the worksheet and started writing down answers.

Ant caught sight of Rosie out of the corner of her eye as Clarissa went up to Mrs Cook's desk to hand in her worksheet. Rosie had a strange expression on her face, as if she was trying to make a difficult decision.

At break, the children crowded round Clarissa, bombarding her with questions. Where was she from? When had she got here? Why had she moved? Did she have any brothers and sisters? What was her favourite colour? Did she like playing tunnel tig?

Rosie pushed through the crowd. "Leave her alone," she said loudly. "It's her first day. You're all too nosy." And Rosie put her arm on Clarissa's shoulder and led her away to the bench in the quiet area. Lucy, Sarah and Rachel stood uncertainly a little way from the bench, talking and glancing at Rosie and Clarissa, who were deep in conversation. From time to time, Rosie laughed, but Clarissa didn't even smile.

Ant watched for a while, to make sure that Rosie was still occupied, then she joined in Emma and Katie's skipping game.

After school, Ant took the boat out to Wishcatchers' Point to check on her wish. She pulled up the creel, but the wish was still there. Should she take it back while she still had the chance? She thought of Clarissa coolly shaking hands with Mrs Cook. Surely a girl like that could cope with Rosie Brash?

She didn't hesitate any longer, but dropped the creel back into the sea. As she leaned over the side of the boat, the shell necklace swung out from under her t-shirt. It felt surprisingly cool as she tucked it back in and her fingers stayed cold all the way back to the harbour.

She tied up the boat and rubbed her chilled hands against her school skirt to get them warm. It was weird that they only felt cold where her fingers had touched the shell. Perhaps it was a sign that she shouldn't have taken the necklace at all. She glanced at her watch. If she was quick, she could take the necklace back to the pool in the elephant rock where she'd found it.

Dumping her schoolbag behind one of the boat sheds, she set out for the stony beach, taking the cliff path this time for speed. She spent ages clambering up and down, but no matter how hard she looked, she couldn't find the elephant-shaped rock.

Chapter 5

Clarissa lay on the floor of her room and tried to concentrate on her homework. After her success with fractions that first day, she had thought she was in for an easy time with her schoolwork. But after a week or so she discovered that although she was ahead in most of the maths, she was behind with reading and she was finding their project on the Victorians difficult because she had come in so late in the topic.

She was supposed to be writing a story from the point of view of one of Queen Victoria's servants, but she kept getting stuck. Did they have ice cream in Victorian times? Clarissa didn't know. She gripped her pencil tightly and concentrated as hard as she could, but it didn't make any difference. In frustration, she threw her homework jotter across the room. It smacked against the wall, then slid down it, falling open on the floor, one corner turned up.

It was stupid homework. It was a stupid project. It was a stupid school.

Clarissa thumped her feet on her bedroom floor. She hated being here. She wanted to go home. She wondered what her old friends would be doing. After school sometimes they had gone into town to have hot chocolate, or to the museum, or to see a film. None of that was possible here. The nearest cinema was nearly an hour's drive away and the nearest museum was the fishing museum in the next village. Even if she wanted to go and look at old nets and floats and boats, there were hardly any buses and she would have to get her mum or dad to take her. There wasn't even a library, just a kind of van with shelves of books in it that came round every two weeks. It didn't have many children's books and most of them were ones she had read ages ago.

True, there was a café, but Clarissa didn't really feel like going for a hot chocolate with anyone from school. And she certainly didn't want to go with Olivia, who was being especially annoying these days. Olivia claimed she loved the new school, her new friends, the new house. She was always saying how glad she was that they had moved.

Just thinking about it made Clarissa want to smash something. Her anger was like a bee buzzing in her head. She felt as if she would explode if she didn't scream or break things.

And then all of a sudden, she was crying. She cried and cried and couldn't stop. She felt so strange and so alone and so unhappy. At first she wept quietly, but then the sobs became louder and louder until she was almost howling. She cried so much and so loudly that she began to frighten herself and that made her cry all the more.

Vaguely, she heard her mum at the door, knocking and saying, "Clarissa, are you all right?"

Ant freewheeled down the hill on her bike, enjoying the way the wind lifted her hair and spread it out behind her. At the bottom of the slope, she swooped left towards home, hardly slowing her pace. It was only when she got to the point just past the Post Office where the road climbed again that she lost speed and started to pedal.

As she passed the Wentworths' house, she heard a strange noise coming through an open upstairs window. It sounded like someone crying hysterically. Ant glanced up at the house and wondered which window was Clarissa's. Then she put her head down and pedalled as hard as she could away and up the hill.

When she got to the crossroads, instead of turning left to go home, Ant went right and cycled down to the harbour. It was getting late and she knew she should be home for dinner or her mum would go mad, but she abandoned her bike and jumped into the boat. Maybe there was still time to take her wish back.

At Wishcatchers' Point she pulled up the creel. The wish was still there. Should she take it back? Ant looked at it for a long time, trying to decide. If it had been Clarissa crying, then maybe she wouldn't be able to cope with Rosie the way Ant had thought she would. But it might not have been Clarissa at all. Ant knew that Clarissa had a sister, Olivia, in Primary Seven – maybe it was Olivia who had been crying. Ant just couldn't imagine Clarissa getting so upset. She was always so calm and unflappable.

Putting the wish back in the plastic box, Ant made her decision. She put it into the creel and dropped it back into the sea. All the way back to the harbour, she tried to ignore the insistent chill of the shell necklace against her skin.

When Clarissa had finished crying, her mum took her downstairs to the kitchen and made her a cup of hot chocolate, in spite of the warm, sunny weather. She even put marshmallows on the top.

Clarissa sipped gratefully. Her eyes felt stiff and washed out and her throat felt tight, but the hot chocolate helped.

Her mum had just started to talk about what they might do at the weekend, when the doorbell went.

"I'll get it," called Olivia from the sitting room, and a few minutes later she came back with Nichol.

Clarissa was glad her mum had made her wash her face. She hoped it didn't show that she'd been crying.

Nichol looked uncomfortable.

"He said he didn't want to come in," said Olivia cheerfully. "But I said of course he should."

"I just brought this," Nichol mumbled, holding out a book.

"Thanks," said Clarissa, pleased that her voice sounded reasonably normal. She looked at the book. It was called *The Victorian Age*.

"That's very kind of you," said Clarissa's mum, smiling at Nichol.

"I just thought it might be useful," said Nichol. "For the essay and stuff."

"It will be," said Clarissa, leafing through the pages. There was a whole chapter on servants and one on Queen Victoria. "It's great. Thanks very much."

"Do you want a hot chocolate, Nichol?" asked Clarissa's mum.

"No thanks," said Nichol. "I need to get back for my tea."

"I'll see you out," offered Olivia.

When she returned, Olivia was grinning widely. "Clarissa's got a boyfriend, Clarissa's got a boyfriend," she chanted.

"Shut up!" said Clarissa.

"Clarissa!" said her mum. "Olivia! Stop it."

"I'm going back upstairs to do my homework," said Clarissa, tucking *The Victorian Age* under her arm.

Olivia climbed onto a kitchen stool and started swinging her legs. "Off to dream about Nichol you mean," she said.

"Don't be so stupid," said Clarissa and went upstairs, stamping heavily on every step.

Chapter 6

Ant didn't realise at first that she was awake. She blinked several times. It was still dark, although her room was softly lit by moonlight coming in through the gap between her curtains.

The singing was faint but unmistakeable. Where was it coming from? Had her mum left the radio on? Ant swung herself out of her bed and padded onto the landing. The new hall carpet felt springy under her bare feet as she stood, her head to one side, listening as hard as she could. Try as she might, she couldn't tell where the singing was coming from. Whichever way she turned, the music seemed to follow her, almost as though it was inside her own head.

Creeping along, she went through the house, searching for the source of the singing. The TV and the CD player in the sitting room were switched off and so was the radio in the kitchen. Peering in through the half-open doorway, she even checked the clock radio in her mum and dad's room, but only the digital clock blinked at her as it counted the seconds. A floorboard creaked as she turned away. She held her breath, but she could see her mum fast asleep in the bed, one arm thrown out across the pillow, the way she always slept when Ant's dad was away on a field trip.

Could the noise be coming from outside? She went to the hall window and peered out across the houses to the harbour. The moon was full and high. The singing seemed to get louder, swelling and dipping inside her head. She moved the plant pot that her mum called "the jardinière" to get close enough to the window to open it.

The night air was cool on her skin when she stuck her head out. The singing rang in her ears, pure and sweet and tantalising. The night was clear and Ant could see hundreds of stars. The longer she looked, the more she felt as if she was being sucked up into the sky. If she only stretched out her arms, surely the sky would take her, zooming her way, way into the velvety black, millions of miles away. She began to feel dizzy and clutched the windowsill, blinking. Maybe she was still asleep after all and the singing was nothing but a dream. But the wood of the sill was solid beneath her fingers and there was nothing dream-like about the feel of the rough patches where the paint had worn away.

A large cloud seemed to sail in from nowhere. In a matter of seconds, it had covered the moon and many of the stars. Ant shivered. She shook her head. The singing had stopped. She listened intently. No, it hadn't stopped. It had just faded until it was almost inaudible.

She closed the window and slid the plant pot back into its place, her mind whirling. Was it the moon that was singing? Or the stars? She remembered something her dad had once told her about some ancient Greek scientist. What was his name? Pie something. Pythagoras, that was it. Her dad had told her that Pythagoras had believed that the stars made music. Had the stars been singing? And if they had, why had she never heard them before?

She tipped her head from side to side, straining to listen, but she could no longer hear the star music. All she could hear was the hum of the fridge, a rustle of bedclothes as her mum turned over, and the beating of her own heart. She went back to bed, pulling the downie right up to her chin. It took a long time to get back to sleep.

Chapter 7

When the bell rang for lunch, Rosie made a beeline for Clarissa as usual and they went to the dining hall together. Rosie usually had school dinners, but since Clarissa had joined the class, she had taken to having packed lunches so she could sit with Clarissa.

"How did you get on with the homework?" asked Rosie, as Lucy and Rachel joined them. Lucy and Rachel too had swapped their usual school dinners for packed lunches, but Sarah's mum said she didn't have time to make up sandwiches.

"Fine," said Clarissa. She didn't like to admit to any problems with schoolwork.

"It took me ages," sighed Lucy. "I'm just no good at essays."

"And the Victorians were so *boring*," said Rosie.

Ant filled her tray with a bowl of vegetable soup, a roll and a glass of milk and started to look for a spare seat. On the days she had school dinners, she always managed to be the last one in the queue and finding a place was often difficult. Today, every seat seemed to have been taken.

Nichol waved at her. His table was full but he pointed to the next one. "There's a space," he said.

It was only when Ant sat down that she realised Sarah was in the next seat. It was too late to move and anyway there wasn't another free place, so Ant started to eat, her stomach churning, hoping Sarah wouldn't speak to her. True, it was normally only Rosie who was horrible to her, but Sarah and the others always went along with it.

She needn't have worried. Sarah seemed just as uncomfortable sitting next to Ant and ate her lunch at double speed before escaping into the playground.

Ant glanced across at Rosie's table. It looked like Clarissa was telling a story. Rosie was laughing. Ant wondered if Rosie was ever horrible to Clarissa. If it *had* been Clarissa she had heard crying the other day, then was it because of Rosie? It was hard to imagine Clarissa ever crying. She always seemed so sensible and so grown-up. She nearly always knew the answer in class and if anyone said something unpleasant to her, she just ignored it. Even when Mrs Cook was having one of her bad-tempered days, Clarissa seemed unfazed. It was as if she had an invisible shield all around her and nothing upsetting could get through it. Surely if Rosie tried to be cruel to her, Clarissa would just laugh it off?

Rosie saw Ant looking and made a face at her. Quickly Ant looked down at her bowl and started scraping up the last spoonful of soup. Since Rosie had had Clarissa to occupy her, she had mostly been leaving

Ant alone, but you never knew when she might pounce. Ant finished her lunch and went outside.

In the playground, Ant queued for a turn on the monkey bars. Nichol was ahead of her. He had his own special technique that nobody else could manage, making a full turn while dangling from each bar. Ant watched him, wondering for the hundredth time how he managed to do it without his arms being pulled from their sockets.

Ant heard Rosie's shrill voice behind her. "Oh look, it's monkey-boy!" Rosie's friends burst out laughing and then they all started chanting, "Monkey-boy! Monkey-boy! Ooh-ooh-ooh!"

Nichol ignored them and finished his turn with a flourish. Ant climbed onto the step, ready to reach out and grab the first bar.

"Where do you think you're going, An-to-ni-a?" said Rosie, in the reasonable voice that meant there was going to be extra trouble.

Halfway to the bar, Ant overbalanced and fell.

Rosie laughed. "I want to talk to you, An-to-ni-a," she said.

"Oh?" said Ant, trying to sound nonchalant as she picked herself up and dusted down her skirt.

"Who gave you permission to sit next to Sarah at lunch?" asked Rosie. She walked right up to Ant. Her face was only centimetres away from Ant's. Ant could see a bit of cress, probably from a sandwich, stuck between Rosie's two front teeth.

"I didn't know I needed permission," said Ant.

"Well, you do," said Rosie, almost spitting the words out. The piece of cress wobbled with every syllable. Ant had the sudden urge to laugh. She bit her lip to stop the laugh coming out.

"Don't you dare make a face at me!" said Rosie. Her voice rose to a shriek.

Ant was just about to protest that she wasn't making a face, when Clarissa intervened.

"Why are you so horrible to Antonia?" she asked.

Rosie was so surprised that she didn't say anything. She just looked at Clarissa in amazement. Clarissa turned away from her and asked Ant, "Can you do the monkey bars?"

Ant nodded.

"Go on. Show me then."

Ant stepped up and swung out onto the bars. Her arms felt like lead, but she managed to get to the end without falling off. When she dropped down, Clarissa was there to meet her.

"That was great. Can you teach me?"

Ant grinned. "I'd love to."

She followed Clarissa back to the start, where Rosie was still standing open-mouthed. Clarissa climbed onto the step. "We didn't have monkey bars at St Mary's," she said. "They look really difficult."

"It's easy once you know how," said Ant. She ignored Rosie, but it didn't mean she didn't feel Rosie's hostile glare burning into her back. "The main thing is to keep going. If you stop you'll fall off."

Clarissa paused, one arm raised ready to reach for the first bar. She looked at Rosie. "Did you know you've got something stuck in your teeth?" she said. Rosie frowned and started to feel around her mouth with her tongue.

Clarissa grabbed the first bar and Ant walked along

beside her, shouting advice. "Swing your legs more ... you can do it ... reach further."

Clarissa fell off after the third bar.

"That was really good for a first time," said Ant. "Do you want to go again?"

Clarissa rubbed at her aching arms. "Maybe tomorrow," she said. She went back to Rosie and the others. They stood, talking and laughing. Rosie's laugh was the loudest of them all.

Ant waited for another shot at the monkey bars. Aware of Rosie and her friends watching, she resolved to make this turn one of her best and gave herself a good swing to start. As she did so, she felt the shell necklace swing out from under her shirt. It bumped on her chest with each bar. When she jumped down, she quickly tucked it back in – but not quickly enough.

Rosie was at her shoulder. "Let me see!" she demanded. She didn't wait for Ant to show her, but slipped her hand under the collar of Ant's shirt and pulled out the necklace. "Oooh, An-to-ni-a. You know you're not allowed to wear jewellery to school. I'm going to tell Mrs Cook." She let the necklace fall and waltzed away, closely followed by her friends.

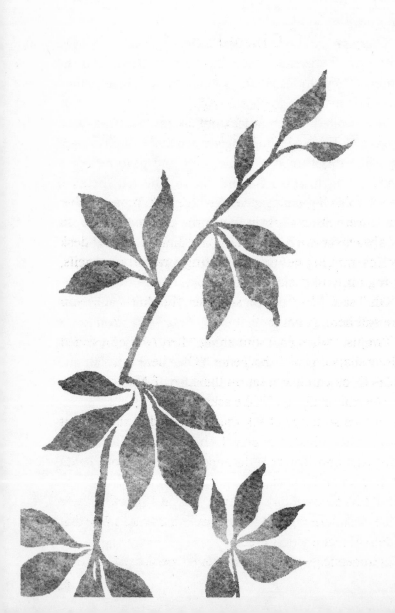

Chapter 8

The school bell rang for the end of the day. Rosie and her friends were always first in line at the classroom door, so Ant always dawdled. She rummaged about in her desk tray, rearranging her things, putting away stray pencils, tidying up worksheets and jotters.

"Oh!" said Mrs Cook in surprise. "I didn't realise you were still here, Antonia."

"I'm just looking for something," lied Ant. She seized a globe-shaped pencil sharpener. "Oh, there it is."

Mrs Cook came and sat on the edge of Nichol's desk. "Is everything all right?" she asked.

Ant was so taken aback that she couldn't think what to say. She rolled the pencil sharpener in her hand, backwards and forwards, hoping that Mrs Cook would just give up and go away.

But Mrs Cook didn't go away. She just perched there on the desk, looking at Ant and smiling a small smile that made Ant feel uncomfortable.

"Is someone giving you a hard time?" persisted Mrs Cook.

Ant shrugged.

Mrs Cook sighed. "Antonia, if you won't talk to me, I can't help you."

"I don't need any help," said Ant. It came out more fiercely than she had meant. She hoped it didn't sound rude.

"If you change your mind, come and talk to me," said Mrs Cook.

"Don't worry, I will," said Ant. She put the pencil sharpener in her pocket, slid the tray under her desk and picked up her schoolbag. She looked at Mrs Cook.

"What is it?" asked Mrs Cook.

"Can I get my necklace back?" Rosie had been as good as her word and reported Ant when they got back after playtime and Mrs Cook had sighed and confiscated the necklace.

"I'd forgotten about that," said Mrs Cook, reaching into her desk drawer. "Here. Please don't wear it to school again, Antonia."

"I won't," mumbled Ant.

"Off you go then," said Mrs Cook.

Clarissa was waiting for Ant at the school gate.

"Hello," said Clarissa.

"Hello." Ant tried not to let her surprise show.

"Do you have to go straight home?" asked Clarissa.

Ant shook her head.

"Do you want to go down to the harbour?"

"All right."

They walked together in uneasy silence. Ant wondered what Clarissa wanted. Clarissa was thinking about how she could put what she wanted to say to Ant.

Clarissa took a deep breath. "You shouldn't let Rosie wind you up like that," she said.

"Like what?" said Ant. She felt her face getting hot. First Mrs Cook, now Clarissa. There were some things she just didn't want to talk about.

Clarissa didn't look at her. She just kept on walking. It made it a bit easier to talk. "Like today when she said you weren't allowed to sit next to Sarah."

"Oh, that," said Ant dismissively. "That's just Rosie."

"You know, she's not that bad," said Clarissa. "She just likes to boss people around."

Clarissa didn't know anything about Rosie, Ant thought. She had never seen Rosie in full flow, reducing younger children to tears, setting even her own friends against each other, making up nasty stories about other children and ensuring that everyone got to hear them. Once Rosie chose someone for her special attention, she wouldn't let go. And this year, it was Ant. Maybe in Primary Seven it would be someone else, thought Ant, scuffing a stone with her shoe as she walked. Only a few weeks to go till the end of term. It would be so much easier staying out of Rosie's way during the summer holidays.

Ant and Clarissa reached the harbour and dumped their schoolbags beside one of the boatsheds before climbing up onto the wall. There was something good about being so high up, feeling the salty breeze on your face. It always made Ant feel better. She ran along the narrow wall to where it stepped up, then turned back to look. Clarissa was walking carefully behind her.

"Come on!" called Ant. "The faster you go, the easier it is to keep to the middle."

"Is it?" said Clarissa doubtfully, but she did increase her speed to a jog. When she reached Ant she was breathless.

Ant turned to climb to the next level, a metre or so higher. Clarissa said, "You're not going right to the end are you?"

"Of course."

"I think I'll just stay here," said Clarissa, in the grown-up voice she used for Mrs Cook.

"Come on," said Ant. "Take my hand and we'll go together."

Clarissa hesitated. She wasn't scared, but she was apprehensive. Like the monkey bars, this was something she hadn't done before.

"I promise I'll go slowly," wheedled Ant.

"OK then."

They climbed up together and walked the length of the harbour wall. The sea surged and slapped against the concrete and it was windier up so high, but Clarissa found she wasn't afraid.

When they dropped down onto the quayside again Clarissa said, "That was fun!"

Ant stuck her hands in the pockets of her school skirt. "You were good," she said approvingly. "The first time I did it, I was so scared my legs were shaking."

"I bet you were about three at the time," said Clarissa.

"I think I was six," said Ant.

"Do you know what amazes me?" said Clarissa.

"What?"

"You can do all this – you know, the monkey bars and the wall and stuff – but you're still scared of Rosie."

Ant's face went stiff. She didn't want to be rude to Clarissa, but she really didn't want to talk about Rosie.

"I'm not scared of Rosie," she said defiantly.

"Maybe scared is the wrong word," said Clarissa.

"But you don't stand up to her."

"She's never made me cry," said Ant. "Not once."

"If you stood up to her, I bet she'd leave you alone."

Ant pretended to be very interested in the mooring ropes of two yachts tied up nearby. "If I was horrible back to her, then I'd be as bad as her," she said.

"You don't need to be horrible," said Clarissa. "Just tell her to get lost."

"I don't think that would work," said Ant.

"It worked for me," said Clarissa.

Ant looked at her in surprise.

"Not with Rosie," said Clarissa. "With a girl at my old school. She kept calling me names. One day I just got fed up and told her to go away and leave me alone. And she did."

"Did she?" said Ant, not convinced. Being called names didn't sound half as bad as what she had to put up with from Rosie. She imagined what Clarissa would do if Rosie started picking on her. She bet Clarissa would start avoiding Rosie too.

Suddenly, Ant remembered her wish. "I've got to go," she said to Clarissa. "I have to check something."

"Can I come with you?"

Ant shook her head. "I need to take the boat and I'm not allowed to take anyone else out without asking."

"Who would know?" said Clarissa.

Ant laughed. Clarissa might know about a lot of things, but she didn't know much about life in a village. Ant's gran always said that in this village even the walls had ears. Whatever you did, wherever you did it, *somebody* you knew was bound to spot you.

"I really have to go," said Ant. She climbed down to

her boat, calling up to Clarissa to throw her the mooring rope.

"Are you really allowed to go out in the boat on your own?" asked Clarissa, clutching the rope.

"I've been doing it for years," said Ant, which wasn't strictly true. It was only recently that she'd finally managed to persuade her parents that she could take the boat out by herself. Even now, much to her disgust, she wasn't allowed to go any further than Wishcatchers' Point.

Clarissa tossed the rope down and stood there, squinting against the sun as Ant coiled the rope and put the oars in their locks.

"See you tomorrow!" called Clarissa.

"See you!" said Ant. She manoeuvred the boat out of the harbour and rowed as hard as she could to Wishcatchers' Point. Out of breath, she hauled up the creel.

It was empty. Her wish had gone.

Ant stowed the creel in the boat and rowed away. At sea the wind was fresh, but her face felt hot, as if she'd been burned by the sun.

Chapter 9

"Now," said Mrs Cook, standing in front of the class with a homework jotter in her hand.

With a jolt in her stomach, Clarissa recognised the jotter.

The class looked at Mrs Cook expectantly, all except Rosie, who was giggling at a note that Lucy had just passed her.

"Rosie Brash!" said Mrs Cook and Rosie jumped. "Now that I have your attention," continued Mrs Cook, "I would like to tell you about a piece of homework which was handed in last week."

Clarissa stared at her desk, wondering what Mrs Cook was going to say. She'd spent ages on that essay. First she'd read Nichol's book on the Victorians from cover to cover and then she'd made lots of notes. Her mum had helped her to think out a good plan and then she'd taken at least an hour to actually write the story. Then she and her dad had gone through it checking for spelling mistakes and missing words.

"This story," said Mrs Cook, waving the jotter, "is one of the best I have read in my whole time as a teacher. Before I tell you who wrote it, I would like to read it to you." Mrs Cook pulled her chair out from behind her desk and sat down.

Clarissa's cheeks were burning, as Mrs Cook started to read.

It seemed to take forever for Mrs Cook to get to the end. Clarissa hadn't realised her essay was so long. Eventually Mrs Cook stopped reading and looked up.

"So, what do you think?" she asked.

"It was brilliant!" said Ant, glancing at Clarissa.

Nichol started clapping, then Emma and Ant joined in. And soon the whole class was applauding, even Rosie.

"Would the person who wrote this please stand up," said Mrs Cook.

Reluctantly, Clarissa got to her feet.

Mrs Cook handed Clarissa her homework jotter. "Well done, Clarissa," she beamed. "Now, I would like you to take this up to Mrs Hardcastle to show her. She's expecting you."

Clarissa was pleased to escape the classroom. It was cooler in the corridor and she felt the heat in her face dying down. The way to Mrs Hardcastle's office passed the toilets and she nipped in and splashed her face with cold water, being careful to keep her jotter dry.

Mrs Hardcastle was very nice about Clarissa's essay and she got Mrs Green, the school secretary to take a photocopy so that it could go up on the "Star Writers" board where everyone could see it.

When Clarissa got back to the classroom, everyone was working on their art project, making Victorian-style greetings cards with doilies and découpage. Clarissa slid into her seat, trying to be as unobtrusive as possible.

Just then Rosie came past carrying a glue pot. "Whoops!" she said, as she stumbled and dropped the pot. Glue splattered down Clarissa's back. Rosie picked up the pot. "Sorry!" she said to Clarissa, but it didn't sound as if she meant it and her eyes were laughing.

Clarissa felt like slapping Rosie. She was sure Rosie had spilt the glue deliberately. She felt the anger rising in her, but then just as suddenly she went very cool.

"It was an accident," said Clarissa. She took off her blue St Mary's sweatshirt and folded it so that the gluey parts were on the inside.

Rosie picked up the glue pot and continued on her way to the sink without saying anything more.

Clarissa put her sweatshirt in her schoolbag and started on her greetings card.

Nichol said, "You should tell Mrs Cook. Rosie did that deliberately."

"I don't think so," said Clarissa and started pasting a picture of a rabbit onto her card.

"Your rabbit's upside down," said Nichol.

Clarissa said, "I know. He's standing on his head."

Nichol laughed. Clarissa smiled at him.

Behind her she heard Rosie whispering to Sarah. "Maybe now she'll stop coming to school in that stupid blue sweatshirt."

Ant heard Rosie too and had seen what happened with the glue. She had a very bad feeling inside. She looked at Clarissa, who was adding glitter to her card now. Clarissa looked so calm but Ant remembered the crying she had heard coming from the Wentworths' house that day and asked herself for the hundredth time why she hadn't destroyed her wish before the Wishcatchers took it.

Chapter 10

Ant tossed and turned in bed. In her dream Rosie had turned into a giant bee and was chasing Clarissa into a corner. Ant tried to save Clarissa, but her feet were so heavy that she could hardly move and when she looked down she had a schoolbag strapped to each ankle. She bent down to undo them, but each time she unbuckled a strap it fastened itself to her even more tightly. With a start, she woke up, panting and sweating.

She got up and went downstairs for a glass of water. As she ran the tap, the power of the nightmare faded. In a way it was even funny – Rosie as a giant bee. Smiling, she sat down at the table with her glass. *Buzz, buzz*, she thought, then jumped as the fridge motor started up unexpectedly. She drank her water, calm now. Outside the window, in the light from the kitchen she could see the branches of the apple tree swaying in the wind. Then she heard it again, that strange, high singing.

She switched off the kitchen light and looked out into the night. Although the sky was clear, there was no moon to be seen, just stars. Could it really be the stars singing? After the last time, she had convinced herself that she had just been dreaming. But now, she was sure that she was wide awake. She unlocked the kitchen door and slipped out into the night.

Above her head, the branches of the apple tree danced, the leaves rustling. She crossed her arms against the cool of the night air and looked up. A new moon. Her dad said sometimes it was called a dark moon. It was strange to think that although she couldn't see it, the moon was still there, hanging in the blue-black sky.

She tried not to think of what had happened at school, but a picture of Clarissa, calmly folding her sweatshirt, kept coming into her mind. Clarissa's face had been so still. She hadn't even frowned. Ant wondered whether Rosie covering her in glue really hadn't mattered to Clarissa – or if Clarissa's stillness hid how upset she was underneath.

Well, one thing was certain. The stars didn't care about any of it. Ant craned her neck and stared at them. Thinking about how old and how far away the stars were made her feel small and unimportant.

She had forgotten about the singing, but it was still there, faint but still audible. Where was it coming from? She went back inside, careful to lock the back door and went back up to her bedroom. Just as she was about to climb into bed, she stopped. There was a strange spot of light just behind the curtains. She didn't remember leaving her torch on – and anyway, she was sure she had put it away in the box under her bed when she'd finished reading under the covers. The only thing on her windowsill was the shell necklace.

Ant rushed over and pulled back the curtains. The necklace was lying where she had left it when she took it off to put her pyjamas on. The shell was glowing with a pale blue-green light. As she stared, she realised that the glow was pulsing in time with the singing. Gingerly, she touched the shell and was surprised to find it cold and damp. When she lifted it, there was a puddle of moisture left on the sill. She put the shell close to her ear and at once her head was filled with the singing, unbearably strong and sweet. Hastily she threw the necklace down. It lay on the carpet, glistening palely, still singing. Ant stood, looking at it, wondering what to do. She opened the window, thinking that she might throw it out, but the thought of it lying there in the flowerbed below all night was more than she could stand. In the end, she wrapped the necklace in a scarf, stuffed it into a shoebox and threw it in the bottom of her cupboard.

She lay awake on her bed for ages, imagining that she could still hear the singing. It was almost light before she managed to close her eyes and get to sleep.

Chapter 11

Ant licked at her ice cream, stopping a dribble from sliding down the cone. Clarissa had already finished hers and was lying on the grass, her head resting on her schoolbag, gazing up into the sky.

Ant looked down to the little bay below and couldn't help seeing the rock where she had sat that day to write her wish.

Rosie was still picking on Clarissa. Every day there was something new. She had taken Clarissa's homework jotter from her tray and dropped it into the sink on top of the paint pots waiting to be cleaned. She had started telling people that Clarissa had a wart on her foot and that whatever they did, they should never go near her gym shoes. She had told Mrs Cook that Clarissa had broken Rachel's pencil deliberately, when in fact Rachel had dropped it and it had rolled under Clarissa's chair and got crushed by accident.

Clarissa didn't seem to be bothered by what Rosie was doing. She had calmly fished her homework jotter out of the sink and cleaned it up as best she could. She had laughed as if it was a huge joke when she heard the story about the wart. She had taken the telling-off from Mrs Cook without a murmur, without even trying to explain what had happened.

But to Ant, Clarissa seemed too cool, suspiciously calm. Ant knew what it was like to be at the receiving end of Rosie's malice. She knew how much it cost not to cry.

The worst thing was that it was all Ant's fault. If she'd never set that wish, then Rosie would still be picking on Ant and Clarissa would still be friends with Rosie. Several times a day, Ant wished that she had destroyed her wish before the Wishcatchers took it – or, even better, that she had never set it at all.

Clarissa sat up and looked down to the bay.

"You know, the day we moved here I saw you down there," she said.

"Did you?" Ant tried to ignore the queasy feeling that rose in her stomach.

"I didn't know it was you then, of course," said Clarissa. "You had the boat tied up beside you and you were doing something funny with a creel."

"Was I?" Ant's hands had gone as cold as her ice cream.

"What were you doing?"

"Oh, just stuff," said Ant.

"What kind of stuff?" Clarissa rolled onto her side and propped herself up on one elbow. She looked at Ant curiously.

"I don't suppose anyone has told you about the Wishcatchers?" said Ant.

Clarissa shook her head.

Ant crunched down the last of her cone and wiped her hands on the grass. She wondered where to start. "It's kind of a secret thing," she said at last.

"I won't tell," promised Clarissa. "I'm very good at keeping secrets."

"Only people who live in the village are supposed to know."

"I live in the village," said Clarissa.

"I know that!" said Ant.

"So what's a Wishcatcher?" asked Clarissa.

"Someone who makes your wishes come true," said Ant. It sounded lame, even as she said it.

"Like a fairy?" said Clarissa.

"A bit," said Ant. "But more – real."

Clarissa's eyes widened. "Tell me more."

"Well," Ant took a deep breath, "say you want to make a wish ..."

"Like to have wings like a butterfly?"

"Any kind of wish. You write your wish on a piece of paper and fold it three times. Then you go down to the harbour and get one of the wishing creels. You put your wish in a plastic box and put it in the creel. Then you have to row out to Wishcatchers' Point and drop the creel."

"What if you can't row?"

"You need to get someone else to take it for you then. Or you can walk to the point and scramble out over the rocks and drop it. But it's a really long way on foot and quite hard going. And it's not a good idea to drop the creel too close to the rocks."

"Why?"

Ant shrugged. "Wishes set too close to the rocks don't come true nearly as often. Maybe they're harder for the Wishcatchers to get to. Or maybe they don't look for them so close to the rocks. I don't know."

"So, once you've dropped the creel, what do you do then?"

"You wait for an answer."

"Do they always come true?"

"Not always. But probably mostly. If you're impatient, you can haul up the creel and check. But you have to be careful! There's a saying: 'A watched wish is seldom granted.'"

"Like 'A watched pot never boils,'" said Clarissa. "We did proverbs at my last school. So what happens to your wish?"

"If your wish disappears from the creel, then it means the Wishcatchers have got it and it's going to come true. If your wish is still in the creel it means the Wishcatchers have rejected it. You can leave it a bit longer if you like. Sometimes a wish isn't granted for ages after it's been set, but that doesn't happen very often. Every couple of weeks, the Wishcatchers bring the used creels back to the harbour." Ant looked at Clarissa. "It's a good idea to bring your own unanswered wishes back though, rather than wait for the Wishcatchers to bring them."

"Why?"

"Just imagine. A creel with your wish sitting in it on the harbour-side for anyone to see. Would you want someone else to know what you were wishing?"

"I suppose it would depend what the wish was," said Clarissa thoughtfully.

"You're not supposed to open other people's wishes,"

said Ant, "but it does happen. If your wish isn't answered after a few days, then it's better to pick it up and destroy it yourself. Rosie Brash is always bringing creels back to the harbour. I don't know what she's wishing for, but it never seems to come true."

"Who can make a wish?" asked Clarissa.

"Anybody who lives in the village. It's mostly children, but sometimes adults set wishes too."

"And if your wish disappears from the creel, it always comes true?"

"Always." Ant squirmed and looked at her watch. "I should be getting home."

"Cool!" said Clarissa. She wondered what she could wish for. Maybe she could wish for Olivia to decide she wanted to go to boarding school. Or for her mum to always say yes every time Clarissa asked for chocolate. "What were you wishing for the day I saw you?" she asked Ant.

Ant was busy re-buckling the straps of her schoolbag and didn't look up. "It was a secret one," she said.

Clarissa thought Ant's voice sounded funny, but she didn't say so.

Ant stood up, shouldering her bag. "What would you wish for?" she asked. "No, don't tell me! Let me guess. You'd wish to move back to your old house and go back to St Mary's."

"You know," Clarissa said in a surprised voice, "I hadn't even thought of that."

They set off down the hill towards the village.

"Does that mean you like it here after all then?" asked Ant.

"I suppose it's not too bad," said Clarissa, with a smile.

Ant deseeded a head of grass with one quick movement and threw the grains over Clarissa's head. "Race you to the bottom!" she shouted.

And the two of them ran down the hill, jostling each other and giggling. They reached the bottom, breathless, and Clarissa took Ant's arm.

"You're a good friend," Clarissa said and Ant felt worse than ever.

That night, Ant took the necklace from the shoebox and put it beside her bed. She stayed awake for ages, but the shell didn't glow and there was no singing. When she couldn't keep her eyes open any longer, she fell asleep and dreamed she was back in the elephant cave. It was dark, but she could just make out a black-gloved hand dropping the palely glowing shell necklace into the pool. As she watched, the rocky floor of the pool cracked open and the necklace slipped into the crevice. The gloved hand made a twisting motion and the water began to bubble and steam. When it went still, the shell necklace had disappeared and there was no sign of the crack which had swallowed it.

Chapter 12

"Clarty!" shouted Rosie. "Hey, you! Clarty Wentworth."

Sarah and Lucy sniggered.

"Just ignore her," said Ant.

"That's what I'm doing," said Clarissa.

They turned their backs and walked down towards the football pitch. Rosie's shrill voice followed them, "Clarty! Clarty! I want to talk to you!"

"Well, I don't want to talk to you," muttered Clarissa. "Why is she calling me Clarty anyway?"

"It means dirty," said Ant.

Clarissa sighed. "She's really beginning to annoy me. I thought she'd have given up by now."

"Rosie doesn't give up easily," said Ant. "She's been picking on me all year."

"Do you know what?" said Clarissa. "If she's going to keep calling me Clarty, I'm going to start calling her Rusty."

Ant giggled. "She'll go mad."

"I don't care," said Clarissa.

Just then, Clarissa felt a slap on her back and Rosie said, "Didn't you hear me, Clarty?"

Clarissa put on an innocent face. "Sorry, Rusty, I was talking to Ant. What was it you wanted?"

Rosie didn't seem to have noticed that Clarissa had called her Rusty. "That's what I wanted to talk to you about. Why are you wasting your time with An-to-ni-a when you could be having fun with us? We're playing pirates and we need someone to walk the plank."

Clarissa looked at Ant. "Do you want to play?" she asked.

Ant shrugged.

Clarissa turned back to Rosie. "Sorry, Rusty. I don't feel like playing pirates and I don't think Ant does either."

"What did you call me?" Rosie faced up to Clarissa.

Clarissa stood her ground. "What did you call me?" she countered.

Rosie held out her hand. "Sarah?"

Sarah handed Rosie her tie. So quickly that Ant didn't even realise it was happening till it was over, Sarah and Lucy each took one of Clarissa's arms and pulled them behind her back. Rosie took the tie and bound Clarissa's hands together.

Clarissa began to panic. She kicked out at Rosie, but Rosie was too quick and caught hold of Clarissa's leg. She twisted it and without her arms to balance her, Clarissa fell to the ground.

"Ahoy me hearties!" said Rosie, gloating. "Man overboard." She dusted down her hands and walked away. "Great fun playing with you, Clarty!" she called over her shoulder. Lucy and Rachel trotted after her, but Sarah hovered, not sure what to do about her tie.

Ant bent down and untied Clarissa. She handed Sarah the tie. Sarah looked uncomfortable. "I'm sorry," she mumbled to Clarissa, before running after Rosie and the others.

Clarissa's knee was bleeding and she had a graze on her elbow.

"We need to go in to Mrs Fletcher," said Ant.

Clarissa shook her head. "I'm fine," she said, but her lip trembled.

"Are you sure?" said Ant doubtfully.

Clarissa sat up. "I just need to sit for a bit."

Ant crouched down beside her. Neither of them spoke for a while.

Ant was wishing that she'd never made that wish. She'd thought it would make things better, but it was far worse watching Rosie torment Clarissa than being on the receiving end of Rosie's cruelty herself.

Clarissa was thinking that maybe it wasn't such a good idea to call Rosie names. Her knee smarted. She checked it for grit, but there didn't seem to be any.

"We should tell Mrs Cook," said Ant.

Clarissa glared at her. "Just like you did when it was you Rosie was picking on?"

"I've never seen her actually hurt anyone before," said Ant. "I think we should tell."

Clarissa shook her head. "No. There has to be something else we can do."

"Like what?"

"I don't know." Clarissa winced as she stood up. She stretched out her leg and tried to put some weight on it.

It hurt a bit, but it wasn't too bad. She began to walk back towards the school.

Ant followed her.

"Maybe we could make a wish," said Clarissa.

Ant's heart thumped as if she'd been running. "I don't think that's a good idea."

"Why not?"

"What would we wish for? You have to be really careful what you wish."

"Why?"

"Things can go really wrong." Ant searched her mind for examples. "Like Lucy," she said. "She wished for a horse and she got one but it turned out that she was allergic to it."

Clarissa laughed.

"It wasn't funny," said Ant. "She couldn't breathe properly and she had to be rushed to hospital in an ambulance. It was really serious."

"What happened to the horse?" asked Clarissa.

"They sold it and got a puppy instead."

"See. It turned out all right in the end then."

The bell rang and Clarissa forgot about her sore knee and started walking faster.

"Wishes don't always come true either," said Ant, trying to keep up. "I've wished loads of times for a sister and that's never happened."

"Just as well," said Clarissa. "You could be stuck with Olivia."

"It's a wee sister I want," said Ant.

Clarissa snorted. "Just look at Tristan."

"He's a boy," Ant pointed out.

"I'm sure a sister that age would be at least as annoying," said Clarissa.

70

They joined the end of the line.

"So," said Clarissa, "are you going to help me make this wish?"

Ant shook her head.

"Suit yourself," said Clarissa airily.

Chapter 13

Sitting cross-legged on her bed, her notepad on her knee and her pencil poised in one hand, Clarissa thought carefully about what she should write. What exactly did she want to wish for? She wanted something to happen to Rosie that would teach her a lesson. Something that would make her realise how awful she was being. Something big enough to make her stop being so nasty.

What could she wish for that would do all that? Maybe she could wish that Rosie's friends would fall out with her. Or that someone would spread a rumour that she wet the bed. Or that someone would start picking on her so that she would know what it felt like.

Clarissa remembered what Ant had said the other day down at the harbour – "If I was horrible back to her, then I'd be as bad as her." Clarissa didn't want to be as bad as Rosie. She just wanted Rosie to stop.

How Clarissa wished that Ant was here to help. Ant was full of good ideas and she was used to setting wishes. She would know what to wish for.

Clarissa stared at the paper and tried to think. She twirled her pencil one way and then the other.

At last she had an idea. She stopped twirling her pencil and wrote:

Dear Wishcatchers,

You might not know me yet. I am called Clarissa and I moved here last month. Rosie Brash is being horrible to me and my friend Ant. I wish that something really embarrassing would happen to Rosie so that she would stop being so sure of herself.

Yours sincerely,
Clarissa B Wentworth

Clarissa folded her wish three times as Ant had told her and put it in her pocket. She told her mum she was going for a walk and set off for the harbour.

As she walked, she tried to remember what else Ant had said about setting wishes. She knew that she had to put the wish in a creel and get it out to Wishcatchers' Point, but she was sure there were some other things she had to remember.

When she got to the harbour, she made for the far side where there was a pile of creels against the wall.

She was just picking up a creel, ready to put her wish in it, when she heard a loud shout.

In surprise, she dropped the creel and looked around. She couldn't see anyone.

"What do you think you're doing?" came the voice again. It was rough and deep and seemed to come from below Clarissa's feet.

Cautiously, she peered over the edge of the harbour. A large, gruff man was climbing the ladder from his fishing boat to the quayside. His hands as they grasped the rungs were enormous and covered in red hair.

"Leave my creels alone!" the man barked.

"Sorry!" said Clarissa, backing away.

The man reached the top rung and waved his fist at her.

Clarissa put her head down and ran. She could hear the man shouting after her, but she didn't stop until she reached the main street. She collapsed onto the bench outside the Post Office and tried to catch her breath.

A few seconds later, Ant plonked herself down beside her. She was panting too.

"Didn't you hear me shouting?" Ant said.

Clarissa shook her head.

"I didn't know you could run so fast!" said Ant, in between gasps. "I saw Peter Chisholm yelling at you. What did you do?"

Clarissa explained about the creel.

Ant started to laugh. "You can't just take any creel, you idiot!" she said.

"How was I supposed to know that?" said Clarissa indignantly.

"You weren't," said Ant. "I'm sorry I laughed. Come

on and I'll take you down to the harbour and show you where the wishing creels are."

She jumped from the bench.

"I'm not going back down there!" said Clarissa.

"Peter was getting ready to go out. He's probably gone by now."

Clarissa still hesitated.

"I'll go and check if you like," said Ant. She didn't wait for an answer, but disappeared round the corner.

In a few moments, she was back. "It's safe. Come on."

Reluctantly, Clarissa slid off the seat and followed Ant back to the harbour.

"There!" said Ant, pointing to a dark corner between two sheds. There was a neat stack of ten or twelve creels. They looked exactly the same as the one Clarissa had tried to take.

"How do you know the difference?" she asked Ant.

"The wishing creels have a sea-urchin shell tied on the inside." Ant showed Clarissa the round, pimpled shells in each creel. "And they're always stacked here." She looked at Clarissa. "How were you going to set your wish anyway? You don't have a boat."

Clarissa shrugged. "I suppose I was going to walk to Wishcatchers' Point."

"All that way with a great big creel bumping on your back?" said Ant.

"You said some people did it," said Clarissa defensively.

"Yes, but only if they're really desperate."

"Maybe I am desperate," said Clarissa in a small voice.

Ant hesitated. You weren't supposed to ask someone what they were wishing for, but she really wanted to know. "Was your wish about Rosie?" she asked eventually.

Clarissa was tempted to say that it was a secret, just as Ant had refused to tell about her wish, but she thought that if she did then maybe Ant wouldn't help her. She nodded and reached in her pocket for the wish.

"It's OK. I don't want to read it," said Ant.

"Go on," said Clarissa. She unfolded the paper and held it out to Ant.

Ant read it and handed it back. "It's a good wish," she said approvingly. "I wish I'd thought of it. Do you want to go and set it now?"

Clarissa shook her head. "I don't think so. Maybe we should leave it for a while and see what happens."

"OK," said Ant. "Do you want to go up to the park?"

They walked back up the hill, talking more about wishes and Wishcatchers.

"I didn't know it would be so hard to get the words right," said Clarissa.

"I know," said Ant. "It's not as easy as you think. You really have to be careful what you wish for."

"Like Lucy and the horse?"

"Yes. Or just imagine that you wished that you could be the best in the class at ballet."

"That sounds like a good wish," said Clarissa.

"But what if your friend was usually the best and then suddenly it was you and she got upset and went home crying. That would make you feel really bad."

"I suppose so," said Clarissa. "Have you ever wished a mistake?"

They had reached the park and sat side by side on the swings, gently rocking to and fro, scuffing their feet with each swing.

Ant bit her lip and swallowed hard.

Clarissa stopped swinging and turned to look at her. "Have you?"

Ant nodded. She scratched an imaginary itch on her arm. "That first day you saw me," she said, "I wished a really bad wish. I kind of knew it was bad when I was writing it, but I set it anyway." Now that she had started telling, she couldn't stop. The words came bubbling up in her throat. "It was a wish about you and I wish I'd never set it. I didn't know you then, but that's no excuse. I wished that Rosie would leave me alone and start picking on you instead." Ant started to cry. "I'm really, really sorry. I should never have wished it."

Clarissa jumped off her swing and put her arm round Ant's shoulder. "It's OK," she said.

"I tried to get it back once we were friends," sobbed Ant, "but it had already gone."

"It's OK," said Clarissa again. "Really, I don't mind. You didn't even know me then. Rosie was being awful and you probably didn't know what else to do."

"I still shouldn't have done it."

"No, you shouldn't," said Clarissa. "But it doesn't really matter. Rosie would probably have started picking on me anyway. She was really annoyed that day about the essay."

"And when you were nice to me at the monkey bars."

"And when I told her she had cress in her teeth." Clarissa grinned. "She didn't like that at all."

"Have you got a hankie?" asked Ant.

"It's a bit grotty," said Clarissa, fishing a tissue from her pocket.

"That's all right." Ant wiped her eyes and blew her nose. "Are you really not angry with me?"

Clarissa narrowed her eyes. "Maybe just a bit," she said. "But I'll forgive you." She gave Ant a hug.

The shell around her neck grew warm and Ant felt suddenly light. The dark, heavy weight she'd been carrying around inside for days had dissolved. She wondered why she hadn't told Clarissa before.

"Now," said Clarissa, "I want to know more about some wishes that have come true."

Ant thought. "I wished for a new friend," she said. "And then you came."

Clarissa gave Ant's arm a playful punch. "Don't go all soppy on me! Tell me some more."

"I wished for a bike for my birthday and I got one. Even though Mum and Dad said they couldn't afford it."

"Any more?"

"I wished for my gran to get better when she was ill and she did."

"I think I'll wish to be the lead in the school play next year," said Clarissa. "I really liked drama at my last school."

"I'm pretty sure Rosie wished for that last year."

"Did she get it?"

"Yes."

"Was she any good?"

"She was actually," said Ant reluctantly.

"What happens if we both wish for the lead?" asked Clarissa. "How do you think the Wishcatchers decide who gets it?"

"I don't know," said Ant. "Maybe they'd make it a play with two lead roles. Like, I don't know, *Hansel and Gretel*."

Clarissa snorted. "Rosie could be Hansel then."

"Or *Beauty and the Beast*," said Ant. "Rosie would have to be the Beauty, obviously."

"Thanks!" said Clarissa. She tried to tip Ant off the swing, but Ant was too strong and held on. Clarissa stepped back, laughing.

Ant jumped off the swing. "Race you to the roundabout!"

Chapter 14

It was too hot to run around, so Ant and Clarissa had joined the group of girls sitting in the shade of the bike shed. Emma was fiddling with Katie's hair, twisting it into lots of tiny plaits. They'd been making Victorian fans that morning and Clarissa had sneaked hers out of the classroom and sat, fanning her face.

They talked about what they were going to do in the holidays. Everybody except Ant and Clarissa seemed to be going away somewhere. Ant never knew when her dad was going to be able to take holiday and they often ended up going away at strange times – at the February break or the October week. Sometimes she even got to miss a few days of school. Clarissa's family wasn't going away this year because her dad had just started his research project at the marine reserve.

"Mum says she might take Tristan, Olivia and me back down south to see our friends there," said Clarissa. "But it's not the same as a proper holiday."

"At least it's something," said Ant, scuffing a stone

with the toe of her shoe. "It better not be for long, though. I'll be so bored while you're away."

"There she is!" Rosie was crossing the playground in large strides, heading straight for them.

"Oh great," groaned Emma and she let Katie's hair fall. She and Katie looked at each other.

"We're just off to the garden," said Katie, getting up.

Emma and Katie walked off, just as Rosie reached the bike shed.

"Hello, Clarty," said Rosie.

"Hello, Rusty," Clarissa couldn't help replying.

Rosie folded her arms and leaned against the bike shed. "I hear you got into trouble with Peter Chisholm," she said.

"Did you?" said Clarissa, trying not to get rattled.

"What were you doing trying to steal his creels?"

"I wasn't."

"That's not what Peter said."

"She made a mistake, that's all," said Ant.

"I wasn't talking to you, An-to-ni-a," said Rosie. "Were you trying to set a wish?"

"I don't think it's any of your business, actually," said Clarissa, trying to keep her voice even.

"I don't believe in Wishcatchers anyway," said Rosie. "It's just a story. It's just your mum and dad picking up the wishes and trying to make them happen. Whatever An-to-ni-a might have told you."

"How come nobody ever sees them then?" asked Lucy, who had followed Rosie across the playground.

"They take the wishes when we're asleep, you idiot," said Rosie.

"If it's just your parents, then what do they do with the wishes?" asked Clarissa.

"If it's *your* parents, Clarty, they probably recycle them," said Rosie scathingly.

"What's wrong with recycling?" asked Clarissa.

Rosie shrugged. "I just don't see why people bother. Having to sort your rubbish into different boxes and all that stuff. It's a waste of time."

"No, it's not," said Ant. "If nobody did it then we would end up living in a great big rubbish dump."

"How many years would it take to get that bad?" scoffed Rosie. "Probably at least a hundred. I'll be dead by then, so why should I care?" She uncrossed her arms. "Anyway, I just came across to tell you not to bother setting wishes. It's an even bigger waste of time than recycling."

"Well, thanks for the advice," said Clarissa, smiling sweetly.

"Come on," said Rosie, and she and Lucy went back to where Sarah and Rachel were giggling by the fence.

Ant felt the muscles in her body go slack. She hadn't even realised that they had tightened up.

"She gave up pretty easily," said Clarissa in surprise.

"She's probably saving herself for something really awful later on," said Ant. "You know, it's weird ..."

"What is?"

"Well, if Rosie doesn't believe in Wishcatchers, why has she been setting the same wish for three years?"

"How do you know that?"

Ant shrugged. "Everybody knows. I've seen her at Wishcatchers' Point loads of times."

"But how do you know she's been setting the same wish?"

"Why else would she keep bringing back the creels before the Wishcatchers do?"

"What do you think she's wishing for?"

"I don't know. To be nice?"

"If it's that, no wonder she keeps setting the same wish. It's definitely not working." Clarissa stretched her legs out in front of her. "Wouldn't you like to know what her wish is?"

"It must be something she really wants," said Ant.

"I suppose we'll never find out," said Clarissa.

But she was wrong.

Chapter 15

When Ant and Clarissa went into the café with Ant's mum, it was much busier than usual and they only just managed to get a table.

"It's never this busy," said Clarissa. "Where have all these people come from?"

"It's Saturday," said Ant.

"So?"

"Haven't you noticed that the village is always chock-a-block at weekends? Especially now the weather's better. Lots of houses here are owned by people who only come down at weekends and in the holidays."

Ant's mum went to order their hot chocolates and Ant and Clarissa sat down at the table. It hadn't been cleared yet, so they pushed the used glasses and coffee cups to one side. Ant wiped cake crumbs from the tabletop with her sleeve.

"Are the holiday-home people allowed to make wishes?" asked Clarissa.

"I don't think so," said Ant. She thought for a

moment. "They wouldn't know about the Wishcatchers anyway. We try to keep it secret."

Clarissa had been thinking about what Rosie said about the Wishcatchers just being your parents. Ant had told her about wishes that had come true, but Clarissa wasn't convinced. It could easily have been Lucy's parents who picked up her wish and decided to buy her a horse. In the same way, Ant's parents could have seen her wish for a bike and bought one for her. Ant had wished for a new friend and that her gran would get better – both of those had come true, but that could just be coincidence. And then there was the wish that Rosie would start picking on Clarissa instead of Ant. That had certainly come true, but the truth was that Rosie would probably have started picking on Clarissa anyway.

"Do you really think Wishcatchers exist?" asked Clarissa.

Ant looked at her in surprise. "Of course! Why else would I keep setting wishes?"

"What if it *is* your parents?" persisted Clarissa. "How do you know it's not?"

"Peter Chisholm wished he was rich and he won the lottery," said Ant. "His parents are dead. And even if they were alive, I'm sure they couldn't arrange for him to win the lottery."

"Peter Chisholm won the lottery?"

"Yes. A couple of years ago."

"So why is he still fishing?" asked Clarissa.

"He got so fed up with people asking him for money and his family fighting over it, that he gave it all away and went back to fishing."

"No wonder he's so bad-tempered," said Clarissa.

"He's all right really," said Ant.

"It could still have been coincidence," said Clarissa.

"What do you mean?"

"Peter winning the lottery. Maybe it had nothing to do with the wish."

Ant shrugged. "I suppose." She thought for a moment. "Nichol's grandad wished to be super-fast when he was younger. He ran all the way into Edinburgh and back in less than an hour."

"That's nearly fifty miles!" exclaimed Clarissa. "Is that really true?"

"Nichol says it is. He says it was in the *Advertiser* and his grandad's still got the article." Ant glanced up at the counter. Her mum was nearly at the head of the queue.

"What do the Wishcatchers look like?" asked Clarissa.

"I don't know. Nobody's ever seen one. At least," Ant leaned towards Clarissa and spoke in a low, dark tone, "nobody's seen one and lived to tell the tale." And then she laughed.

"Now you're just kidding me on," said Clarissa.

Ant shrugged. "It's true that nobody's ever seen one. Or if they have, they're not letting on."

"I wonder what would happen," mused Clarissa, "if you sneaked down to the harbour at night and waited till the Wishcatchers brought the creels back."

"What a great idea," said Ant. "You're a genius! How come I never thought of that before?"

"You would have to wait until the pile of wishing creels was low," said Clarissa, thinking her plan through.

"And you might end up waiting a few nights before they came," said Ant.

"You'd need to put on warm clothes," said Clarissa.

"In this weather?" Ant protested. "It gets a bit cooler at night and maybe a bit damper, but it won't be cold."

"OK, maybe just put on a fleece or something. And you'd need some food, to keep you going."

"And there would need to be two of you, so you could keep each other awake," said Ant.

Clarissa looked at her. "Did you think I would do this on my own?"

"Of course not!" said Ant. "Are we doing it, then?"

"Doing what?" said Ant's mum, putting the tray with the hot chocolates down on the table.

"Nothing," said Ant.

Behind Ant's mum's back, Clarissa nodded her head emphatically.

Chapter 16

When the alarm clock started to beep, Ant jumped. She fumbled around under her pillow for the off switch. In her rush to get at it, she knocked the clock onto the floor with a clunk. The beeping got louder. Quickly, Ant rolled out of bed and switched it off. She knelt on the floor, her breath coming out loud and harsh, waiting to see if her mum would come in to see what was going on. She waited for what seemed like ages, but she didn't hear any movement from her mum and dad's room.

Very carefully, she got up and put on her clothes. She took her torch from under her bed and the rucksack she had packed earlier with chocolate, her water bottle and a notebook and pen. She wasn't quite sure if she would need to write anything down, but it was better to be safe than sorry, as Mrs Cook was fond of saying.

She glanced at the shell necklace on her windowsill. It was glowing slightly, but as far as she could tell, it wasn't singing. Her hand hovered over it. Should she take it? Usually it made her feel better when she put it on, but she didn't like the thought of wearing it when the shell was damp and glowing. And what if it started to sing when she and Clarissa were trying to hide? She left the necklace where it was, stuffed her torch in her pocket, put on the rucksack and picked up her shoes. Very slowly, she opened her bedroom door and crept down the stairs.

At the front door, she took the keys from their hook, grasping them firmly in her fist so that they wouldn't jingle.

It was only when she was safely outside in the moonlit night that she put on her trainers. As she headed for the Wentworths' house, she wondered if Clarissa would be waiting as they had arranged. Clarissa was often late for school because she had slept in and Olivia had told Ant once that Clarissa could sleep through anything. As Ant walked along the empty street, spooky in the yellowy light of the streetlamps, she wondered if she would be brave enough to go to the harbour on her own if Clarissa hadn't woken up.

But she needn't have worried. When she got to the gate, there was Clarissa, crouched down in the shadow of the hedge.

Before Ant could speak, Clarissa put a finger to her lips and signed to Ant that they should move along the street. When they got to the park, she stopped and whispered, "That was close! Tristan woke up when I was going down the stairs and I had to bribe him with a biscuit to get him to go back to bed. I kept thinking that he was going to go and wake Mum and Dad."

They walked down to the harbour, keeping away from the streetlights as much as possible. The tide was high and they could hear the insistent sound of the sea whooshing against the cliffs.

Ant had been right, it wasn't cold, but Clarissa still couldn't help shivering.

"Stay still!" hissed Ant. She flattened herself against the wall of Peter Chisholm's cottage and pulled Clarissa in beside her. A metre or so away, someone passed them. It was too dark to make out who it was. The same thought occurred to them both: was it a Wishcatcher? Just then, whoever it was whistled and a small, black dog scurried from the bushes and went to heel. The person and the dog walked on.

"What a weird time to take your dog out!" whispered Clarissa.

"Come on," said Ant.

There were fewer streetlamps down at the harbour and, even with the full moon, it was easier to find dark corners to hide in. The place was deserted, with nobody to disturb them.

"We should go between that shed and the stack of fish boxes," said Clarissa. "That way we can see the entrance to the harbour and the place where the wishing creels are both at the same time."

"OK," said Ant.

They carefully took the top fish box from the pile and turned it upside down to make a seat. Then they pushed it in as far as they could and sat down, huddling together.

The moonlight had been swallowed up by a bank of cloud, but the longer Ant and Clarissa sat, the more their eyes adjusted to the gloom. Before long, they could make out the bulky shapes of the fishing boats moored in the harbour and the dark hulk of the lifeboat shed. Close by they could hear the tug and suck of the calm water within the harbour and further away the rush and boom of the waves breaking on the rocks.

For a long time nothing happened.

Ant suppressed a yawn.

"I was sure it would be tonight," Clarissa whispered. "There are only two wishing creels left."

"Shh!" said Ant. "Listen."

Clarissa screwed up her eyes and listened hard, but she couldn't hear anything new. "What is it?"

"A boat engine. It's turning towards us."

Clarissa listened again and very faintly she could just catch the steady *chug, chug, chug* of an engine somewhere out on the water. They pulled as far back as they could on their fish box. Ant found that she was holding her breath and had to force herself to breathe normally.

A van came down onto the other side of the harbour, driving right to the end before cutting its lights and its engine.

"It's probably just a boat coming in with a catch," Ant whispered into Clarissa's ear.

She was right. The boat came into the harbour and tied up. Two men got out of the van and helped to unload the fish boxes from the boat. Ant and Clarissa could hear the loud voices of the fishermen and the men from the van, swapping stories about the day's catch and the price they might get for it. There was a lot of laughter.

"They might be a bit quieter," hissed Ant. "People are trying to sleep."

"Not you I hope," whispered Clarissa, yawning again.

"Not yet, but if we don't spot a Wishcatcher soon, I'm not sure I can stay awake."

"Me neither."

The van reversed up the harbour at top speed, turned noisily and sped off up the road.

Ant wriggled off her rucksack and took out her chocolate. She broke off a few pieces and gave some to Clarissa.

"That's a bit better," whispered Clarissa, letting a square of chocolate dissolve on her tongue.

They sat for a while longer, watching the harbour so hard that their eyes started going starry and they kept having to blink.

"I don't think it's going to be tonight," said Ant, through a large yawn.

"My bottom's gone numb," said Clarissa, shuffling as she tried to get comfortable.

"Let's go home and try again tomorrow," said Ant.

As quietly as they could, they picked up their bags and slid from their hiding place.

"Look!" hissed Ant, pointing. "It's beginning to get light."

Sure enough, over the headland Clarissa could just see the faintest grey creeping into the blackness of the sky. They started to climb the hill to the village, still keeping to the shadows when they could.

At the telephone box, they stopped and turned to take one last look at the harbour. To their surprise, they saw the lights of another boat approaching the harbour entrance. They ducked between the wall and the telephone box and peered out, hardly daring to breathe.

As the boat drew nearer, they understood why they

hadn't heard its engine as it approached. It was a yacht, with its sails up. Ant waited for the sails to come down as it got closer to the harbour. Yachts usually furled their sails and came in on their engines because it was difficult to navigate the narrow harbour entrance otherwise. But this boat kept coming with its sails raised. It came in fast and straight. There must be a good sailor at the helm, Ant thought. She wished she had brought her binoculars.

The boat was strung with multicoloured lights that twinkled and there was a faint sound of music that got stronger as it came into harbour. It wasn't a tune that Ant recognised, but she found herself humming along to it all the same. It was a slow, sad melody, which swelled and grew and then faded away, just like waves on open water.

The boat moored and finally the sails were furled, just as the music stopped. Suddenly the harbour lights went out. Ant gasped and Clarissa clutched her arm. They blinked, trying to adjust to the sudden dimness.

A procession of coloured lights was moving along the quayside. Ant counted five, six, seven lights. They swayed from side to side as they approached the place where the wishing creels were kept. Surely this must be the Wishcatchers, Ant thought.

Just then the moon emerged from behind a cloud and Ant and Clarissa could make out seven figures, dressed in what looked like long cloaks which billowed behind them. Each carried a lantern with a coloured light in one hand and three or four creels tied together slung over the opposite shoulder. The group paused close to where Ant and Clarissa had been hidden just a short time before and unloaded the creels, neatly stacking them in two piles.

When they had finished, the Wishcatchers huddled together for a moment, their cloaks tangling together in the breeze. Everything went very still and Ant and Clarissa could hear their own heartbeats loud in their ears. Then the Wishcatchers put out their lamps and started to walk swiftly up the hill.

Ant clutched at Clarissa. "Come on!" she hissed. "We have to get out of here or they'll see us as they go past."

They scrambled from their hiding place and slid round to the other side of the wall. Crouching, they moved as fast as they could to the end of the street, not daring to look back. When they got round the corner, without a word, they began to run. Ant didn't pause at Clarissa's gate, but gave a quick wave as Clarissa darted into the garden. She kept running, her rucksack bumping on her back. Glancing behind her she saw the dark shapes of the Wishcatchers coming round the corner. Taken aback, she stumbled and went over on her ankle. She only just managed to crawl into the bushes at the front of Etta Chisholm's garden before the Wishcatchers came past. Wide-eyed she peered at them through the hedge.

The Wishcatchers walked with a smooth, unhurried gait, their hooded black cloaks billowing behind them. Their feet were silent on the pavement and Ant checked to make sure their shoes actually touched the ground.

Glancing up again, she saw something that took her breath away. Round the neck of the Wishcatcher closest to her, she could see a shell necklace, exactly like the one she had found in the cave. The shell was glowing pale green and Ant could just make out the faint sound of singing.

It was all over in seconds. The Wishcatchers swished past her and went on their way, leaving Ant wedged into the hedge, twigs prickling her head, wondering if she really had just seen what she thought she had. It was only when her foot started to get pins and needles that she extricated herself from the bushes and walked the last couple of metres to her house.

She fumbled with the keys. Why had she bothered to lock the door? It seemed to take ages to get it unlocked and get inside.

As she climbed the stairs to her room, she was breathing so heavily she was sure she would wake up her mum. She paused on the landing to listen, but there was no sign of movement.

At her bedroom door, she stopped, with one hand on the handle. She had a sudden conviction that the necklace was gone, that while she was out the Wishcatchers had come and claimed it, but when she went in, the necklace was lying where she had left it on her windowsill. The shell glowed softly green, but even as Ant looked, the glow faded, getting fainter and fainter until only the pale gleam of a normal dog-whelk shell remained.

Hesitantly, Ant took the necklace in her hand. The shell felt cold and moist. As she held it, the damp seemed to evaporate, fizzling away in her hand. She put the shell to her ear, but there was no singing. The air in her room rang with the absence of sound, as if there had been singing, but it had now stopped and the air was not sure how to fill the gap that was left.

Still clasping the necklace in her hand, Ant looked out of her bedroom window. The harbour lights had come back on and the sky was brightening, but even so she couldn't tell if the Wishcatchers' boat was still there. She got her binoculars from under her bed and took another look. There was no sign of the boat, not in the harbour, nor anywhere on the sea. How could it have disappeared so fast?

Ant heard a noise from her mum and dad's room, a creak of the bed and then footsteps. Her mum must have woken up. What if she decided to come in and check on her?

Quickly Ant stuffed her rucksack under the bed, kicked off her shoes and jumped under the covers, still fully clothed.

She heard the creak of her mum's bedroom door. She lay very, very still. The handle of her own door turned and she heard her mum come in, tiptoeing around the felt pens and books and schoolbag strewn over the floor. She felt the soft touch of her mum's lips on her cheek and the soothing of her mum's hand on her forehead. Suddenly she wanted to sit up and tell her mum all about the necklace and the Wishcatchers. She even opened her eyes a fraction, but when she saw her mum's face through her eyelashes, she stopped. If she told her everything, her mum would be angry. Ant had been out at night when she should have been asleep. She'd walked to the stony beach by the rocks when she'd been told countless times not to. *And* she'd gone into the elephant cave when her mum had warned her never ever to go into a cave without an adult. Ant firmly closed her eyes again. No, it was better to keep her secret.

Chapter 17

Ant's mum pushed her mermaid lunchbox across the table towards her. "Can you put this in your schoolbag please?" she said. She frowned. "I can't find your water bottle anywhere."

It was still in Ant's rucksack under her bed. "I took it upstairs," she said, trying to sound normal.

"What on earth did you do that for?" asked her mum.

Ant shrugged.

"Well, don't just stand there. Go and get it. You'll be late for school!"

Ant was glad to be out of the kitchen. She ran upstairs and got the water bottle. It was still full from the night before, so she stuffed it and her lunchbox into her schoolbag and went back downstairs.

"I'm off!" she shouted in the hall.

"Wait a minute!" called her mum from the kitchen.

Oh no, Ant thought. She knows I was out last night and she's going to tell me off.

Her mum came out of the kitchen, wiping her hands

on a dishtowel. "Don't forget your money for the trip. It's on the table."

Ant had completely forgotten that today was their class trip to Carnburgh Castle. She groaned. Now she would have to unpack her lunch and put it in her rucksack. There was no way she was carting her schoolbag plus her books and pencil case round the castle. She picked up the money and put it in her pocket, then trekked back up the stairs.

"Remember your waterproof!" her mum shouted up the stairs. "It looks nice now, but you never know what it's going to be like later."

"Better safe than sorry," said Ant in her best Mrs Cook imitation. She packed her rucksack and went back downstairs.

"I'm really off now," she said.

"Wait a minute!" called her mum again.

This is it this time, thought Ant. But all her mum said was, "Remember to go straight to Gran's after school," and gave her a kiss and a hug before waving her off.

Ant and Clarissa ignored the singing competition that Rosie and her friends had started from the back of the bus and whispered to each other about what had happened the night before.

"I nearly woke the whole house up when I got in," said Clarissa. "I knocked the lamp off the hall table. It sounded like a bomb had gone off."

"Did you break it?"

"I don't know how, but it didn't smash. I stood there

for ages, holding my breath, but everybody just slept through it."

"The back of the bus canny sing, canny sing, canny sing," shouted Nichol and Emma and Katie with the others at the front of the bus.

"Did you get back all right?" Clarissa asked.

Ant nodded. She had never told Clarissa the story of the shell necklace. It had seemed so weird that she was sure Clarissa would think she was making it up, but after what had happened the night before, she felt the urge to share her secret. "You know that shell necklace I've got?" she said.

Clarissa nodded.

"One of the Wishcatchers was wearing one just like it." Ant told Clarissa how she had found the necklace in the waterfall pool and how she'd never managed to find the elephant cave again.

Clarissa's eyes widened. "You know," she said, "it sounds more like that necklace found you than you found it."

Ant thought about this. "You think I was meant to find it?"

"Don't you?"

"But why?" Ant wondered aloud.

"I don't know. But I bet it's got magic powers."

Ant stared at her. "Well, there are some strange things about it." She told Clarissa about the glowing and the singing and the strange clammy coldness. "And last night, it was almost like the shell on the Wishcatcher's necklace was singing to my shell. Like they were talking to each other."

"Wow!" said Clarissa. "I wonder what it all means."

"I wish I knew," said Ant.

The noise of the singing grew much louder as Rosie and her friends at the back of the bus took their revenge. "The front of the bus canny sing, canny sing, canny sing."

Clarissa groaned. "I wish they'd shut up. They're giving me a headache."

Ant's head throbbed too. It wasn't surprising considering she had hardly slept at all. She yawned widely and beside her Clarissa yawned too.

"I don't know how I'm going to stay awake today," Ant said.

At the castle they got off the bus and hung around waiting for their guided tour to start. Ewan and Nichol were messing about near the ramparts. Ewan got up on the top and wobbled exaggeratedly, while Nichol pretended to swipe at him with his bag.

"Go on, Nichol. Knock him off!" teased Ant.

Nichol turned to look at her, bag poised, "Should I?"

Several of the class chorused, "Yes!"

"Should I?" asked Nichol again, still with his bag raised, ready to swing.

"Yes!" More of the class joined the chorus this time.

Just then, Mrs Cook came out of reception with one of the castle guides. "Nichol MacIntosh! Ewan Dowie! Get down immediately and stop messing about. Now, follow me."

The boys got down, grinning, and the rest of the class fell in behind Mrs Cook and the guide.

Ant nudged Clarissa. "Did you see Rosie's face?" she asked. "She was white as a sheet when Ewan was up there."

"Maybe she fancies Ewan and she thought he was really going to get pushed over."

"The only person Rosie fancies is herself," said Katie, coming in on the conversation.

The tour guide started talking and Ant didn't say anything more, but she saw Clarissa looking at Rosie curiously.

When they stopped for lunch, Clarissa took Ant aside. "I was watching Rosie all morning," she said. "She kept as far away as possible from the ramparts. I think she's scared of heights."

"I didn't think Rosie was scared of anything," said Ant.

They sat on the grass, eating their lunch. Clarissa had just taken a bite out of her sandwich when it was snatched from her grasp. She turned to see who had taken it and saw Sarah running away, brandishing the sandwich in one hand. Rosie was laughing as she called over, "Just doing a healthy lunch check. Mrs Hardcastle's orders."

Clarissa didn't stop to think. She was on her feet and over to where Rosie was sitting in a split second. To Rosie's surprise, Clarissa snatched the egg roll she was holding and ran off with it.

"Just doing a check on yours!" Clarissa shouted.

Rosie chased after her.

Clarissa climbed onto the ramparts.

Rosie stopped dead.

Clarissa waved the roll. "Come and get it!"

Ant watched, a funny feeling growing in her insides.

"Go on, Rosie!" yelled Sarah and Lucy.

Rosie was like one of the marble statues they'd seen earlier in the castle, just as pale and just as still.

"Scaredy cat!" shouted Ewan.

At this, Rosie took a couple of steps towards the rampart. Ant could see that she was trembling.

Clarissa waved the roll. "It looks tasty. Maybe I should just eat it."

Rosie was right at the rampart now. She put one foot up on the edge. Her face was whiter than ever.

"Clarissa Wentworth!" came Mrs Cook's voice. "I'm surprised at you. Get down at once."

Clarissa jumped down. "Sorry, Mrs Cook," she said.

"Is that your roll?" asked Mrs Cook.

Clarissa shook her head. She handed the roll back to Rosie.

"Apologise to Rosie," said Mrs Cook.

"Sorry," said Clarissa, but she didn't look at all sorry. She wiped her floury hands on her skirt and went back to sit with Ant, who was unwrapping a melting KitKat.

Rosie made a big show of taking the roll between the tips of her thumb and first finger and dumping it in the bin. "Eww!" she said pointedly. "I'm not eating it after she's touched it." She went off to wash her hands.

Clarissa grinned at Ant. "Did you see her face? She's not just scared of heights, she's petrified."

Ant didn't answer. She tried to blot out the picture of Rosie's terrified face by concentrating on licking every last smudge of chocolate from her fingers.

Chapter 18

When they got back to school after their trip, Clarissa asked Ant, "Do you want to come round to my house?"

Ant shook her head. "I've got to go to my gran's."

She walked Clarissa as far as her gate, then doubled back and headed for her gran's house, scuffing a stone with her shoe as she went along. To get to her gran's you could go through the village or across the beach. Ant decided to go by the beach, vaulting the wall and dropping down onto the shore. It took longer that way, because it was slower going on the sand, but she wanted the extra time to think.

She couldn't stop remembering Rosie's white face as Clarissa taunted her from the rampart. It was the first time she had seen Rosie lose her cool and it made her feel strange.

Ant ran down to the tideline and looked for flat, smooth stones. When she'd found half a dozen, she put down her schoolbag and started to skim them. Her first stone jumped three times before sinking into the water. The second only skipped twice, but by the time she got to the last stone, she managed six jumps. Wishing Clarissa had been there to see her prowess, Ant shouldered her bag and trudged through the sand to her gran's house.

In good weather Ant's gran always left her door open and Ant went in without knocking, shouting, "Hello, Gran!" to announce her arrival.

She found her gran in the kitchen, taking off her dough-smudged apron. On the worktop was a wire rack full of cooling chocolate-chip biscuits.

Her gran gave her a kiss. "Did you have a good trip?"

"It was OK," said Ant.

"Are you hungry?"

"Starving!"

Her gran surveyed the biscuits. "That's good. I need somebody to help me eat these."

Ant grinned. "That sounds like a job for Super-Ant!"

Her gran went to fill the kettle. "Well, that's a load off my mind. I was wondering how I was going to manage to eat them all by myself."

Ant sat down at the table and grabbed a biscuit. It was warm and chocolatey and delicious. "Mmmm," she said, wiping crumbs from her chin.

Her gran handed Ant a glass of milk and made herself a cup of tea. "So," she said, sitting beside Ant at the table, "tell me what's new with you."

Ant shrugged. "Not much." But she couldn't stop thinking about the adventure of the night before and her nagging questions about the shell necklace and the Wishcatchers. She picked up her glass and drank some of her milk.

"Not much," repeated her gran, sipping tea from her favourite blue stripy mug.

Ant hesitated. "Can I ask you something?" she said.

"Of course." Her gran took a biscuit and started to eat it while she waited for Ant's question.

"How much do you know about Wishcatchers?"

Her gran considered. "Not as much as some people, but more than a lot of people," she said eventually. "What do you want to know?"

"What do they wear?"

"I'm not sure. I've never actually seen a Wishcatcher. But people say they wear black cloaks and carry lanterns."

"What about jewellery?"

"Jewellery?" said her gran in surprise.

"You know, rings and necklaces and things. Like, do they wear necklaces with shells on them?"

Her gran looked at Ant shrewdly. "What makes you ask that?"

Ant shrugged. "No reason."

Her gran pursed her lips and raised her eyebrows.

Ant looked down at the table, using her finger to trace the grain of the wood.

Her gran sipped her tea. It seemed a long time before she spoke and Ant squirmed in the silence. "I've heard," said her gran eventually, "that the Wishcatchers wear necklaces with dog-whelk shells."

"Creamy-white ones?"

Her gran nodded. "Is there anything you want to tell me?" she asked.

Ant hesitated. She knew she could trust her gran with a secret. Once, Ant had broken one of her mum's favourite vases, a blue one with starfish on it. Her gran had helped her to sweep up the mess and had taken Ant to the pottery in the next village to buy a replacement – all without Ant's mum knowing a thing about it.

"I think I found a Wishcatcher's necklace," said Ant.

All her gran said was, "Mmmm," but it was an encouraging "mmmm" so Ant went ahead and told her the whole story about the elephant cave and the pool and the waterfall and about going out late to spy on the Wishcatchers. "So," she finished, "do you think it is a Wishcatcher's necklace?"

"Yes, I think it probably is. Have you noticed anything unusual about it?"

"Sometimes it glows and gets damp," said Ant. "And sometimes it sings."

"At a spring tide?"

Ant hadn't thought about this. "I don't know," she said.

"Well, when did it glow?"

"Last night."

"It was a spring tide yesterday."

"Was it?"

"Of course. It was a full moon."

Ant had noticed the moon but she hadn't paid attention to the tide. "Is it always a spring tide at a full moon?"

Her gran gave an exasperated sigh. "Antonia Cowan, don't tell me you've lived your whole life by the sea and you don't even know the first thing about tides!"

Ant suddenly found the bottom of her glass very interesting.

"I despair of your parents! I despair of your teachers! What on earth do they teach you in school these days?"

Ant shrugged. "We just did the Victorians."

Her gran snorted. "The Victorians! Do you think there weren't any tides in Victorian times?"

Ant shrugged again. She'd never really thought about it.

Her gran put down her mug. "You do know what a spring tide is?"

"A really high tide," Ant muttered.

"And how often do you get them?"

Ant shrugged.

"Twice a month," said her gran. "Once at a full moon and once at a new moon."

"Oh," said Ant. She thought about the nights she had heard the shell singing and tried to work it out. "That sounds about right."

"Of course it's right. I didn't get to be this old and wrinkly without learning a thing or two."

Ant grinned. "No, I mean about the shell. It sang last night and the time before was about two weeks ago."

"I thought so," said her gran. "Your great-gran used to tell me stories about a girl who found a Wishcatcher's shell. She always used to say that by the light of a full moon, by the dark of a new, the Wishcatcher's shell would make its music."

Ant shivered. "What happened to the girl? In the stories, I mean."

"Too many adventures to tell you in one go," said her gran with a smile. She glanced at the clock. "Your mum will be here any minute."

"Tell me one," pleaded Ant.

"Another time," said her gran. "Now, I need to put the rest of these biscuits away and start getting my tea ready."

Ant got down the biscuit tin. It was round with a picture of a soppy-looking girl with a pink floppy bow in her hair.

"Do the Wishcatchers really have special powers?" she asked, as she stacked biscuits in the tin, two at a time.

"Of course they do," said her gran. "How else would they make the wishes come true?"

"Rosie Brash says it's just your mum and dad," said Ant.

"What do you think?"

"When I wished for a bike, Mum and Dad already knew that I wanted one, so they could have just gone out and bought it."

"That's true," said her gran. "And I'm sure a lot of the wishes people set are like that – things they think might come true without a wish, but they want them so much that they set a wish to be on the safe side."

"When you were ill, I wished for you to get better."

"I didn't know that. Thank you!" Her gran hugged her. "That wish certainly worked."

"But you might have got better anyway," said Ant.

"I suppose I might have," said her gran. "But the doctor said it was a miracle. He'd never seen anybody as ill as I was get better so quickly."

Ant put the lid tightly on the tin. "I made a really bad wish," she said.

Her gran was busy at the sink, peeling carrots. "Did it come true?" she asked.

"Yes," said Ant in a small voice. "But I wish I'd never set it."

Her gran scraped peelings into a sheet of newspaper. "I don't know an awful lot about it," she said, "but the way I understand it, the Wishcatchers think very carefully about each wish before they decide what to do about it. So there must be a reason why the Wishcatchers granted your wish."

"I wish I knew what it was," said Ant gloomily.

"Could you pop these on the compost heap?" Her gran held out the newspaper parcel of peelings.

Ant took them. "I wish I was a Wishcatcher," she said.

"Be careful what you wish for!" said her gran.

"What do you mean?"

"Don't you think being a Wishcatcher must be a huge responsibility?"

"If I was a Wishcatcher," said Ant, "then I could find out what Rosie's been wishing for."

Her gran opened the fridge to get out some mince. "Why don't you just ask her?"

Ant laughed. "She'd never tell *me*."

"Why do you want to know anyway?"

Ant shrugged. "I just do."

Chapter 19

It was Clarissa who had discovered the perfect space for a den in the bushes beside the park. The gorse bushes on the outside were prickly, but if you didn't mind the odd scratch, you could push your way through to the rhododendrons beyond. There was a gap big enough for Clarissa and Ant to sit, with the thick, dark leaves making a perfect roof above them. They had made a small hollow in the ground and covered it with a layer of old leaves, and on top of that they'd spread a travelling rug that Clarissa had borrowed from her garage.

On Saturday afternoon, they had taken a picnic in with them – Hula Hoops and Party Rings and apples – and were sitting in their den, munching and chatting about what they were going to do over the summer. They had eaten the crisps and biscuits and Ant was just about to cut up the apples with her penknife, when they heard voices in the field behind them.

"Stop whingeing! It can't be that sore. You're pathetic!" said a boy's voice.

They could hear someone crying, the sharp, thin kind of crying you do when something is hurting you. Then there was the harsh sound of a slap.

"I'm warning you! Shut up! You're doing my head in!"

The crying faded to a whimper, but didn't stop.

Ant and Clarissa squirmed round in their hiding place and wriggled closer to the edge of the bushes, so that they could see who it was. Careful not to get jagged by the thorns, they each found a gap to peer through.

To their surprise, they saw Rosie Brash being almost dragged along by her brother Lewis.

Lewis looked furious as he stomped along, muttering insults. "Pig-face!" he said.

Rosie was crying and her face was red where Lewis had slapped her. She stumbled and Lewis hauled her roughly to her feet.

"Ow!"

Lewis slapped her on the leg. "Shut up, donkey-breath. Someone will hear."

Ant looked at Clarissa and Clarissa looked at Ant. They crawled out of the den and slipped under the fence into the park.

"Race you to the swings!" Ant shouted loudly.

Out of the corner of her eye, she could see Lewis jump. He let go of Rosie and walked away, his hands in his pockets. Ant and Clarissa waited until he was out of sight before they climbed the fence into the field.

They found Rosie sitting behind the bushes, blowing her nose on a dirty tissue.

"Are you all right?" asked Clarissa.

"Why should you care?" said Rosie. "Leave me alone."

Clarissa held out a clean tissue. Rosie snatched it from her and wiped her eyes.

Ant crouched down beside Rosie. "We saw what happened with Lewis."

"It's none of your business," said Rosie fiercely.

"We're just trying to help," said Clarissa.

"I don't need your help," said Rosie.

"Why was he being so awful to you?" asked Clarissa.

"He said I broke his phone," said Rosie. "But I didn't even touch it." She got up, stuffing the tissues in her pocket.

They started to walk, Ant and Clarissa on either side of Rosie. She didn't tell them to go away.

"You should put some arnica on your cheek," said Clarissa. "It looks like it's going to bruise."

Rosie put a hand to her cheek. "Good," she said. "Maybe this time Mum will believe me. She always takes Lewis's side. He lies and lies, but she always believes him."

They came to the end of the field. Rosie stopped. "You won't tell anyone, will you?"

"Of course not," said Ant. She looked worried. "Is there anything else we can do?"

Rosie shook her head. "He's just so much bigger and faster than me. If only I was bigger than him. Or if I could fly – then I could escape easily." She smiled a weak smile. "But there's not much chance of that, is there?"

A thought suddenly struck Ant. "That's what you've been wishing for all these years, isn't it?"

"Don't be daft," retorted Rosie. "I don't believe in Wishcatchers."

"But I've seen you, loads of times, out at Wishcatchers' Point."

Rosie glared at her. "You know you're not supposed to ask people what they wish for," she said. "It's private."

"Sorry," said Ant, but she didn't sound very apologetic.

Clarissa changed the subject. "Do you want to go and get an ice cream?"

"No, thanks," said Rosie. "I'm going to go home and tell Mum what happened." She fingered her cheek. "Lewis will probably have calmed down by now."

"Well, see you on Monday," said Clarissa.

"See you," said Rosie. Ant and Clarissa watched her walk away. She looked small and alone.

"Are we going to get that ice cream then?" asked Clarissa.

"We'd better get the stuff from the den first," said Ant and they went back towards the park.

Chapter 20

"I think I've worked out what Rosie keeps wishing for," said Ant.

"Oh?" said her mum. They were driving to the station to pick up Ant's dad, who was just back from his latest research trip, which had finished unexpectedly early. This time, he was supposed to be at home for a few weeks. Ant had been so excited about seeing him, but the episode with Rosie had put it right out of her mind.

"I think she wants to be able to fly," said Ant.

Her mum shot her a sharp look via the rear-view mirror. "What makes you think that?"

"Just something Rosie said." Ant ran her fingers up and down the webbing of her seatbelt, enjoying the bumpiness of the rough ridges against her nails.

"Did you ask her?" Ant's mum fiddled with a knob on the dashboard and the air in the car got cooler.

"Not exactly," said Ant. "Mum, is there a reason the Wishcatchers can't grant the wish to fly?"

Her mum indicated to turn right and waited for a break in the traffic. Ant waited for a reply.

"It's a very big wish," said her mum eventually.

"So it could never come true?"

"I'm not sure I would say never," said her mum. "But, as far as I know, it's unusual for supernatural wishes to be granted."

"But not impossible?"

Her mum thought for a moment. "Josie Holton wished that she could be in two places at once. Her son was in hospital in Glasgow for a big operation and her daughter's baby was due in Australia. She knew they both needed her, but she didn't see how she could help them both, so she wished that for a week she could be in both places at the same time."

"And that came true?" asked Ant.

"Yes. She's got photos to prove it."

"Wow!" said Ant. "That's amazing. It would be so cool if you were invited to two parties at the same time and you could go to them both."

Her mum laughed. "I'm not sure the Wishcatchers would think it was worth granting a wish just for that. Josie's wish was for an important reason."

"Rosie must have an important reason for setting the same wish for three years."

"I'm sure it's not just about perseverance," said her mum. "It must be more complicated than that."

Ant turned to look out of the window. A transporter, with six or seven cars on it, thundered past, scuffing up dust and grit. "I would really like Rosie's wish to come true."

"Oh?" said her mum in surprise. "I didn't think you liked Rosie."

"I don't." Ant was silent. It was difficult to put into words why she wanted Rosie to have her wish granted, when Rosie had been so nasty to her. She thought of Rosie's tear-stained face in the field by the park and remembered the way she had felt the day Rosie had forced her into playing sleeping princesses. That day, when she had felt alone and unhappy, she had imagined a seagull swooping up and up and away and it had helped. How much better it would be to actually zoom into the air and soar away! No wonder Rosie kept wishing to be able to fly. That way she could escape from Lewis any time she wanted.

They pulled into the station car park. As they got out of the car, Ant said, "Is there no way that I could help Rosie's wish come true?"

"Well," said her mum as they walked towards the station, "I've heard it said that it helps if more than one person makes a wish. It reinforces the wish." She looked at Ant. "But I still don't understand why you're so keen to make Rosie's wish come true."

Ant shrugged. How could she tell her mum that she felt sorry for Rosie because she knew exactly how if felt to be picked on? She'd never told her mum just how miserable Rosie had made her. And she'd promised Rosie not to tell anyone about Lewis.

"I mean, do you really think she deserves it?" asked her mum.

Ant nodded. Her mum raised her eyebrows but didn't say anything. They were standing on the platform now. There were clocks everywhere, but Ant's mum still looked at her watch. "Two minutes till Dad's train," she said. "Perfect timing!"

They looked expectantly along the platform. Ant got butterflies in her stomach the way she always did when her dad was coming home. She thought the sound of a train coming in was one of the most exciting sounds in the world, especially if her dad was on it.

It seemed a very long two minutes, but suddenly the train was there, filling the space Ant had been staring at for so long. Her dad was one of the first off. He had a big backpack over his shoulder and a huge holdall in one hand, which he put down so that he could give Ant a hug.

"Dad!" said Ant. "Don't squeeze so hard!"

Her dad let her go and gave her mum a long hug instead.

All her mum said was, "I'm not sure I like the beard, Neil." But she was smiling that special smile she kept just for him. She scooped up the holdall in one hand. "Come on!" Ant took one of her dad's hands and her mum took the other. They walked towards the car together, swinging their arms happily.

That night, Ant lay awake. Since her conversation with her gran, she'd been paying attention to the moon and the tides. It was a new moon tonight which meant a spring tide, so if her gran was right, the shell should start singing.

She yawned. Why was it so hard to stay awake when you wanted to and yet when you were really tired sometimes you couldn't get to sleep at all? She reached under her bed for her torch and got out her book. Maybe reading would help her stay awake.

She woke up to find the book on the floor and the torch still clutched in her hand. She switched it off and went to check on the shell. Sure enough it was faintly glowing, and as she strained her ears she could just make out the singing. The shell was damp in her hand. As she watched, the glow got brighter and the singing got louder. She put it to her ear, half-expecting to hear the rushing-sea sound you usually hear when you listen to a normal shell, but the sea sound was drowned out by the singing.

It was sweeter and clearer than ever and as she listened, she began to make out what sounded like words. They weren't in any language that she recognised. After a while, she realised that there was more than one shell-voice singing. It was as though her shell was singing and then several other shells answered. She wondered what they were saying to each other. Had the Wishcatchers realised a necklace was missing? Were they trying to find the lost shell?

Ant parted the curtains and stared out into the night. She looked for a long time, but there was no sign of a Wishcatcher coming to reclaim the necklace. In her hand, the shell paled and fell silent. Ant put it back on the windowsill, crawled into bed and slept. She dreamed again of the elephant cave, but this time, there was no necklace to be found. In her dream she searched and searched the bottom of the pool to no avail. She woke in a panic, convinced that the Wishcatchers had come and taken the necklace while she slept. But the necklace was still where she had left it, pale and silent, on the windowsill.

Chapter 21

Clarissa and Ant sprawled on the floor of Clarissa's bedroom, writing wishes in their best handwriting.

"Do you think if we decorate the wishes it might give us a better chance?" asked Clarissa.

"I don't know. It's worth a try," said Ant.

Clarissa got out her art box. It was full of glue and sequins and feathers and stickers and jewels. They spent a long time getting the wishes looking just right.

At last Ant sat back on her heels. "That's mine finished."

"Mine too."

They looked at their wishes, sparkling and shining with glitter and hologram stickers. They had both written the same wish before signing their names:

Dear Wishcatchers,

I really, really, really, really, really,

really, really, really, really, really, really wish that you would make Rosie Brash's wish come true. You might not think it, but she does deserve it and it would make her very happy.

"Right," said Ant, "let's go and set them."

They had already been down to the harbour to check that there were wishing creels left. Clarissa had wanted to know what happened if they were all gone, and Ant had told her that you just had to wait for the Wishcatchers to bring some back. But luckily there were plenty of creels today.

They stood on the quayside and studied the creels.

"They say that some are luckier than others," said Ant, picking at some leftover glue that had stuck to her fingers.

"How do you know which ones are the lucky ones?" asked Clarissa.

"The ones that look most used," said Ant. "They're the ones that have had most wishes come true."

"Like this one?" said Clarissa, lifting up a creel with a fraying rope and blackened base.

"Exactly like that," said Ant. She too chose an old and battered creel. They put their wishes in the plastic wishing boxes and then into the creels before taking them down to Ant's boat.

It was hard carrying the creels down the ladder to the boat and Clarissa almost overbalanced. It wasn't much better in the boat itself. Clarissa had never been on a boat that small before and she was a bit wobbly at first.

"Don't we have to put life jackets on?" she asked nervously.

"I suppose so," said Ant, who didn't always bother with one if she thought she could get away with it. "They're under the seat." While Clarissa struggled with her life jacket, Ant shrugged hers on impatiently, got the oars into the rowlocks and started out for Wishcatchers' Point.

Clarissa tried not to show how queasy she felt. The sea was glassy and calm but she still felt every slight dip and rise. It seemed ages until Ant stopped rowing and said, "Let's drop them here."

Clarissa said, "Here goes!" managing to sound heartier than she felt.

"One, two, three!" counted Ant. On three they dropped their creels into the sea with hardly a splash. Ant noted the position and colour of the buoys so that they could check up on them later.

"Wouldn't it be good if our wishes came true?" said Clarissa.

"We just need to wait and see," said Ant. "Mum says they don't often grant wishes that ask for magical powers and things like that."

"I think they will," said Clarissa confidently. "There's no way the Wishcatchers will be able to resist such beautiful wishes!"

"Let's hope so," said Ant. Under her t-shirt, she could feel the comforting warmth of the shell necklace and she took this as a good sign.

Chapter 22

It was gala day and Ant and Clarissa were arm in arm, walking along to the main street. Bunting was strung above their heads and the high-school band was playing "Dancing Queen". Behind them, Ant's dad was singing along and her mum groaned and said, "Neil, must you?"

There were people everywhere, all trying to find the best place to stand to see the floats when they went past.

Rosie went by with Sarah, Lucy and Rachel. Clarissa expected her to say, "Oh there's Clarty and An-to-ni-a," and shout something nasty at them. But she didn't. She just gave Clarissa and Ant a small smile, as if she was embarrassed, and went on her way.

They found a good spot on the corner opposite the Post Office and Ant and Clarissa stood right on the kerb, their toes almost in the road, to make sure nobody could come and stand in front of them and spoil their view. Clarissa's mum and dad joined them. Clarissa's dad had Tristan in a carrier on his back.

"I wish I could go up there," said Clarissa, tickling

Tristan's dangling foot. "Then I'd be able to see everything."

"You're far too heavy for that!" said her dad, ruffling her hair.

Clarissa squirmed away, smoothing her hair. She took out her clasp and put it back in again. Ant fiddled with the shell necklace, which she was wearing hidden under her t-shirt as usual.

"Here they come!" said Clarissa's mum, pointing along the street.

The first float came into view and everybody cheered. It was decorated in paper flowers and bits of coloured netting and big bows. On it were crammed lots of girls from the dance school, dressed in leotards and ballet skirts, with their hair scraped back into buns. The float moved along the street very slowly, so the dancers could dance – although the little ones didn't actually dance at all. They just jumped up and down and waved at their mums and dads.

The next float had the local jazz band on it and as it got nearer the noise of sliding trombones and smooth saxophones drowned out the school band on the hill. Behind the girls, Ant's dad sang along:

"Oh when the saints,

oh when the saints,

oh when the saints go marching in."

Behind the jazz band came a whole line of floats: the Brownies wearing homemade owl masks, travelling in a float done up with paper trees and an astroturf floor; the karate club in their white suits, practising their moves; the lifeboat crew in a huge papier-mâché replica of the lifeboat; the members of the Rotary Club, dressed as fishermen through the ages and throwing sweets into the crowd. The procession went on and on.

Clarissa caught a sweet and gave it to Tristan.

"Here comes the gala queen!" said Ant.

The queen was chosen by the children in third year at the high school and she had six ladies-in-waiting. Every year, the queen and her ladies had different dresses. Last year the queen had been in pale blue and her ladies in blue and white spots. This year the queen was Emma's big sister, Hannah, and she was wearing a pink dress with a big skirt covered in lace and sequins.

"Doesn't she look lovely!" said Clarissa.

"Mmm," said Ant. Actually, Hannah in that big puffy skirt reminded Ant of the plastic lady with the knitted dress that her great-gran kept in her bathroom to cover up the spare toilet roll.

The ladies-in-waiting were in lilac dresses embroidered with tiny white daisies. The queen sat on her silvery throne and the ladies-in-waiting sat around her, waving at the crowd.

"I thought she would have a crown," said Clarissa, disappointed.

"She hasn't been crowned yet," said Ant. "The float will take her down to the harbour-side and last year's queen will crown her. Come on, let's go."

They joined the throng of people making their way down to the harbour, where a stage and loudspeakers had been set up in the car park.

A man in a suit had the microphone and was making a speech that seemed to go on forever. Ant and Clarissa stopped listening and looked around. Emma and Katie waved at them from the roof of the shed where they had perched for a better view. Mrs Cook walked by and they tried not to catch her eye. They spotted Sarah, Lucy and Rachel, sitting on the grass, eating ice cream and giggling, but Rosie was nowhere to be seen.

On the stage, last year's queen had taken a glittering tiara from a velvet cushion and was putting it on Hannah's bowed head. Everyone clapped and cheered.

A different man in a similar suit took the microphone and started making a speech every bit as boring as the first one. The adults tried to look interested, but the children started to drift away. Ant and Clarissa wandered over in the direction of the wishing creels.

"I wonder if Rosie's wish will ever come true," said Clarissa.

They had been checking the creels at least once a day, but each time they looked the wishes were still there.

"Talking of Rosie, there she is," said Ant, pointing.

Rosie was with Lewis and they were talking. Ant and Clarissa were too far away to hear what was being said, but Rosie didn't look happy. Ant could feel the shell round her neck become colder and when she put a hand up to touch it, she found that it was damp. She was filled with dread.

Suddenly Rosie started to run and Lewis chased her. He was bigger and faster and each way Rosie turned, Lewis cut her off.

"Stop, Lewis!" Rosie shouted. "Let me past!"

Ant could see what was going to happen. "He's going to make her go up on the wall!" she said.

"She'll be terrified," said Clarissa. "We have to stop him."

They started to run.

But Lewis already had Rosie cornered. With a desperate look on her face, Rosie turned to the harbour wall, back to Lewis, then back to the wall. She really didn't want to climb, but she couldn't see how else she could escape.

Lewis lunged at her and she scrabbled upwards, her feet slipping on the concrete. On the top she wobbled, but she regained her balance and started running. Meanwhile, Lewis ran to the other end, climbed up in a flash and started towards her.

Rosie's face was white. She trembled. The tide was in and spray slapped the seaward side of the harbour. She looked at Lewis, who was gaining on her fast. He was too fast for her. Even if she turned and ran back the way she had come, he would catch up with her. She looked around wildly for some way of escape.

Clarissa was in a panic. "She's going to jump!"

Sure enough, just as Lewis drew close to her, Rosie leapt off the wall towards the sea. Ant found herself clutching the shell necklace as she rushed over. The shell felt strangely warm and reassuring, but Ant didn't have time to think about what that might mean.

Ant and Clarissa heard Rosie's scream, but they didn't hear either a thud or a splash to tell them whether Rosie had fallen onto the rocks or into the sea.

Lewis was shouting Rosie's name, his voice hoarse and panicky. Tears were streaming down his face. When Ant and Clarissa reached him, he was whispering, "I didn't mean you to fall in, Rosie," over and over. Ant pulled herself up onto the wall.

"Look!" she yelled.

Clarissa scrambled up to join her and followed the

line of Ant's pointing arm. She gasped. Rosie wasn't lying hurt on the rocks below. She wasn't splashing and spluttering in the fizzing sea. Instead, she was hovering a metre or so above the water.

Clarissa looked at Ant. Ant looked at Clarissa. They grinned and gave each other a high five.

They looked again at Rosie. She had her eyes tightly shut and she was shaking.

"What are you afraid of?" shouted Ant above the noise of the waves.

"She's scared of heights, you idiot!" hissed Clarissa.

"But there's no way she can fall if she can fly!" Ant shouted, loudly enough for it to reach Rosie. She was still gripping the shell and she felt it pulse in her hand, like a heartbeat.

Rosie opened one eye. She dipped one shoulder and flew to the right. She opened the other eye. She kicked with her legs and gained height. Her eyes widened. She kept climbing and climbing and then suddenly turned and dive-bombed down, whooping in delight. At the last minute, she banked and climbed again.

"Wooo-hooo!" she called.

Ant looked at Lewis. He had sat down on top of the wall, his head in his hands and he was sobbing. "I didn't mean it," he was saying. "I didn't mean it."

Ant tapped him on the shoulder, but he didn't look up. She crouched down beside him. "Lewis, look at Rosie."

"I don't want to see," he said. "Is it really bad?"

Ant pulled him to his feet. "Look!" she said, giving him a shake. "Look!"

Lewis looked.

Rosie flew straight towards him, her tongue sticking out. Inches away from him, she turned and swooped away, laughing.

"See you later!" she called, and with that she took off and flew away, to Wishcatchers' Point and beyond.

Ant and Clarissa stood watching the flying Rosie become smaller and smaller, a tiny dark shape still shrinking, a black dot until she finally disappeared from view altogether.

"I can't believe we just saw that!" said Clarissa.

Ant shook her head. "Me neither."

The two girls stared out to sea, their necks craned until they ached, their eyes straining until they started to smart.

Lewis picked himself up from where he had slumped on the harbour-side and slunk away without a word.

Back at the crowning ceremony, nobody seemed to have noticed the drama on the quayside. The speeches had finished and Hannah and her ladies-in-waiting were posing for yet another round of photographs.

The school band began to play "One day I'll fly away". Ant and Clarissa looked at each other and started to howl with laughter.

The gala queen and her ladies-in-waiting were rounded up and put back on their float to do one last tour of the village before the gala party started at four o'clock.

Ant and Clarissa stayed on the harbour, sitting cross-legged on top of the wall. Neither of them said it, but they were waiting for Rosie to come back.

"Look!" said Ant at last, spotting something in the sky that was the wrong shape for a plane or a seagull. "There she is!"

Rosie landed neatly on the pier and rubbed her goosebumpy arms. "It's chilly up there," she said. "Next time I'll remember to take a jumper."

"What was it like?" asked Clarissa.

"Amazing!" grinned Rosie. "Brilliant! Fantastic! Unbelievable!" Her smile faded. "Is Lewis all right?"

"He'll be fine," said Clarissa. "He just got a bit of a shock."

"Serves him right," said Ant.

"I couldn't agree more," said Rosie.

Ant and Clarissa jumped down from the wall.

"Never mind about Lewis," said Ant. "Tell us more about the flying. We want to know everything!"

As they headed for the village and the gala party, Ant and Clarissa pestered Rosie with questions and Rosie tried to answer them as best she could. Ant had tucked the necklace back under her t-shirt and she could feel its comforting warmth as they walked, arm in arm, Rosie in the middle, with Ant and Clarissa on either side.

Chapter 23

"Right, children," said Mrs Cook, clapping her hands. "Get into groups of three or four."

Around the gym hall, the children milled about, sorting themselves into groups.

"Antonia? Clarissa? Where's the other member of your group?"

Ant shrugged. Clarissa said, "It's just the two of us, Mrs Cook."

"Can I have a volunteer, please, from a group that already has four?" asked Mrs Cook.

To everyone's surprise, Rosie put her hand up.

"Thank you, Rosie."

Sarah, Lucy and Rachel stared as Rosie crossed the gym hall to join Ant and Clarissa.

"Now, here's what I want you to do," said Mrs Cook.

Afterwards in the playground, Ant said, "That was a bit weird."

"I know," said Clarissa. "Weird but good."

Rosie passed by with her friends.

"Hi Rusty," said Clarissa.

Rosie stuck out her tongue. But then she grinned, in a friendly way, before sauntering over to the monkey bars.

Ant shook her head. "I'm not sure I can get used to this!"

"You're never happy," said Clarissa. She glanced at Ant, who was fiddling with the shell necklace. "I thought you weren't going to wear that to school any more. If Mrs Cook sees it you'll be in trouble."

"It doesn't seem right to leave it at home," said Ant. "I feel like I need to look after it ..." She hesitated. "It's like it – speaks to me."

"But you said you didn't understand the singing."

"It's not that. It's more like – it tries to tell me things. When I set that wish about Rosie picking on you, it went all cold as if it didn't like what I was doing. And when Rosie was being horrible to me, it would feel warm and reassuring, as if it was telling me that everything would be all right."

"That could just be coincidence," said Clarissa. "Or maybe it was ..."

"Just my imagination? Then how come I found it in my hand when Rosie fell off the harbour wall? I wasn't even thinking about it. I was too busy watching Rosie."

"Did it do anything? Like go shivery to warn you Rosie was going to fall?"

"That was the strange thing. It went all warm and soothing. It was like it knew Rosie's wish was going to come true."

Clarissa stared at her, open-mouthed.

"What is it?"

"You don't think it was you? I mean, could it have been you holding the necklace that made the wish come true right then?"

Ant pulled her hand sharply away from the necklace. "I – I don't think so," she said. "Wishes come true because the Wishcatchers take them from the creels."

"But what if there's another stage we don't know about?"

Just then, the bell rang for the end of playtime.

Standing behind her in the line, Clarissa whispered in Ant's ear, "I told you before. I think you were meant to find that necklace."

Under her school shirt, Ant felt the shell warm against her skin. She put up a hand to touch it. So much had happened since the day she had found it in the cave in the elephant rock. She had made a new friend. She had discovered some of the Wishcatchers' secrets. She had seen a spectacular wish granted right in front of her eyes. And now, most unexpectedly of all, Rosie Brash had actually started being nice to her. Whatever happened, Ant felt sure that the summer holidays were going to be full of adventure.

If *you* could make any wish, what would it be?

You can write your favourite wish for yourself and your best friend here.

To: the Wishcatchers

My wish:

From:

Why not decorate your wish like Ant and Clarissa do in the book? You never know ... it might come true!

To: **The Wishcatchers**

My friend's name:

My wish:

From:

You can share your wishes with us by emailing
kelpies@discoverkelpies.co.uk or sending us a letter. Your
wish could be featured on the Discover Kelpies website
discoverkelpies.co.uk.

Author interview: Carol Christie

Q: What inspired you to write The Wishcatchers?
Carol Christie [CC]: One day I was walking along the harbour at St Abbs, in the Scottish Borders, and I saw a pile of creels. I just started to wonder what would happen if you put wishes in them and dropped them out at sea – and that's when the idea of *The Wishcatchers* popped into my head.

Q: Have you always wanted to be an author?
CC: I knew I wanted to be a writer when I was about eight or nine, and I wrote my first novel when I was ten.

Q: What were you like when you were in primary school?
CC: I was the kind of kid who would read the cereal packet if there wasn't anything else to read. I was always reading and writing stories and poems – but I also really liked to play chasing games in the playground with my friends.

Q: Have you ever been picked on like Antonia in The Wishcatchers?
CC: I was lucky that there wasn't a Rosie Brash in my class at school! But I think everyone has times when they feel other people are getting at them. People can be unkind, often without meaning to – and we can be unkind to others too, even to our friends.

Q: Who is your favourite character from The Wishcatchers *and why?*
CC: That's quite a hard one, but I think in the end I'd have to say Ant, because she's funny and tends to jump in without thinking about the consequences. I think Clarissa would be a good friend to have though, and I have a sneaking admiration for Rosie's inventiveness.

Q: Did you base the characters on anyone you know in real life?
CC: Ant is her own person, as she would be the first to tell you, and not exactly like anyone else. However, there are some things she has in common with my own daughter and some of her friends – and she's also a little bit like me.

Q: Apart from The Wishcatchers, *which book would you advise all children to read before they grow up?*
CC: It's really hard to choose just one book, but if I absolutely have to, I'd say *The Secret Garden* by Frances Hodgson Burnett.

Q: If you had three wishes what would they be and why?
CC: My first instinct was to wish to always be happy. But then I thought that if everything always went well, I wouldn't learn much. It's never fun when bad things happen to you, but often these are the times that make you better and stronger, so I don't think I could really wish them away. Instead, I'm going to wish, like Rosie, that I could fly. I'd also like to be able to speak any language. And I'd love to live in a house that cleaned itself so I wouldn't have to do it!

Lari Don

Helen and her fabled beast friends face treacherous tasks and dangerous monsters in three thrilling adventures.

First Aid for Fairies and Other Fabled Beasts

Wolf Notes and Other Musical Mishaps

Storm Singing and Other Tangled Tasks

Janis Mackay

Join half-selkie hero Magnus Fin on two exciting
underwater adventures as he struggles to save
the sea and his selkie family.

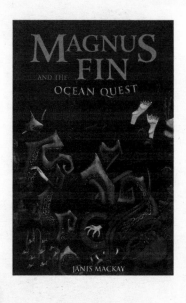

*Magnus Fin and the
Ocean Quest*

*Magnus Fin and the
Moonlight Mission*

Has your favourite book got all this?

excitement magic adventure

thrills danger

legends friendship

battles

Discover your NEW favourite book at...

discoverkelpies.co.uk

Read exclusive extracts and author interviews, sign up for the Kelpies newsletter and enter fantastic competitions.